"I don't know why, Mr. Ryecart. It's not as if I could fire *you.*"

Lucas made an  not what I mea... you forget our r... single moment?"

"No, since you ask... ...get. Neither would you, I imagine, if you were in my position."

"Underneath me?" he suggested.

"Yes!" She'd walked right into it.

"If only you were." His eyes made a leisurely trip down her body and back again. The elevator arrived and Lucas stepped in with her. Tory wanted to step out again, but it seemed an act of cowardice. What could he do in the five seconds it took for the elevator to reach the ground floor?

He could hit the emergency button. Tory didn't realize that was what he'd done until the elevator lurched to a halt.

"You can't do that!"

He grinned. "For now, let's talk."

"I don't want to talk."

He drawled, "Fair enough. Let's not talk." And with one step he closed the distance between them....

It used to be just a nine-to-five job...

until she realized she was

Now it's an after-hours affair!

Getting to know him in the boardroom...
and the bedroom!

Available only from Harlequin Presents®

Coming next month:
His Boardroom Mistress
by
Emma Darcy
#2380

Alison Fraser

THE BOSS'S SECRET MISTRESS

In Love With Her Boss

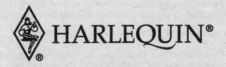

HARLEQUIN®

TORONTO • NEW YORK • LONDON
AMSTERDAM • PARIS • SYDNEY • HAMBURG
STOCKHOLM • ATHENS • TOKYO • MILAN • MADRID
PRAGUE • WARSAW • BUDAPEST • AUCKLAND

ISBN 0-373-12378-7

THE BOSS'S SECRET MISTRESS

First North American Publication 2004.

Visit us at www.eHarlequin.com

Printed in U.S.A.

CHAPTER ONE

'LUCAS RYECART?' Tory repeated the name, but it meant nothing to her.

'You must have heard of him,' Simon Dixon insisted. 'American entrepreneur, bought up Howard Productions and Chelton TV last year.'

'I think I'd remember a name like that,' Tory told her fellow production assistant. 'Anyway, I'm not interested in the wheeling and dealing of money men. If Eastwich needs an injection of cash, does it matter where it comes from?'

'If it means one of us ending up at the local job centre,' Simon warned dramatically, 'then, yes, I'd say it matters.'

'That's only rumour.' Tory knew from personal experience that rumours bore little relationship to the truth.

'Don't be so sure. Do you know what they called him at Howard Productions?' It was a rhetorical question as Simon took lugubrious pleasure in announcing, 'The Grim Reaper.'

This time Tory laughed in disbelief. After a year in Documentary Affairs at Eastwich Productions, she knew Simon well enough. If there wasn't drama already in a situation, he would do his best to inject it. He was such a stirrer people called him The Chef.

'Simon, are you aware of your nickname?' she couldn't resist asking now.

'Of course.' He smiled as he countered, 'Are you?'

Tory shrugged. She wasn't, but supposed she had one.

'The Ice Maiden.' It was scarcely original. 'Because of your cool personality, do you think?'

'Undoubtedly,' agreed Tory, well aware of the real reason.

'Still, it's unlikely that you'll fall victim to staff cuts,' Simon continued to muse. 'I mean, what man can resist Shirley

Temple hair, eyes like Bambi and more than a passing resemblance to what's-her-name in *Pretty Woman*?'

Tory pulled a face at Simon's tongue-in-cheek assessment of her looks. 'Anyone who prefers blonde supermodel types... Not to mention those of an entirely different persuasion.'

'I should be so lucky,' he acknowledged in camp fashion, before disclaiming, 'No, this one's definitely straight. In fact, he has been described as God's gift to women.'

'Really.' Tory remained unimpressed. 'I thought that was some rock singer.'

'I'm sure God is capable of bestowing more than one gift to womankind,' Simon declared, 'if only to make up for the many disadvantages he's given you.'

Tory laughed, unaffected by Simon's anti-women remarks. Simon was *anti* most things.

'Anyway, I think we can safely assume, with a little judicious eyelash-batting, you'll achieve job security,' he ran on glibly, 'so that leaves myself or our beloved leader, Alexander the Not-so-Great. Who would you put your money on, Tory dearest?'

'I have no idea.' Tory began to grow impatient with Simon and his speculations. 'But if you're that worried, perhaps you should apply yourself to some work on the remote chance this Ryecart character comes to survey his latest acquisition.'

This was said in the hope that Simon would allow her to get on with her own work. Oblivious, Simon remained seated on the edge of her desk, dangling an elegantly shod foot over one side.

'Not so remote,' he warned. 'The grapevine has him due at eleven hundred hours to inspect the troops.'

'Oh.' Tory began to wonder how reliable the rest of his information was. Would Eastwich Productions be subject to some downsizing?

'Bound to be Alex,' Simon resumed smugly. 'He's been over the hill and far away for some months now.'

Tory was really annoyed this time. 'That's not true. He's just had a few problems to sort out.'

'A *few*!' Simon scoffed at this understatement. 'His wife

runs off to Scotland. His house is repossessed. And his breath smells like an advert for Polo mints... We do know what that means, Goldilocks?'

At times Tory found Simon amusing. This wasn't one of them. She was quite aware Alex, their boss, had a drink problem. She just didn't believe in kicking people when they were down.

'You're not going to do the dirty on Alex, are you, Simon?'

'*Moi?* Would I do something like that?'

'Yes.' She was certain of it.

'You've cut me to the quick.' He clasped his heart in theatrical fashion. 'Why should I do down Alex...especially when he can do it so much better himself, don't you think?'

True enough, Tory supposed. Alex was sliding downhill so fast he could have won a place on an Olympic bobsleigh team.

'Anyway, I'll toddle off back to my desk—' Simon suited actions to his words '—and sharpen wits and pencil before our American friend arrives.'

Tory frowned. 'Has Alex come in yet?'

'Is the Pope a Muslim?' he answered flippantly, then shook his head as Tory picked up the phone. 'I shouldn't bother if I were you.'

But Tory felt some loyalty to Alex. He had given her her job at Eastwich.

She rang his mistress's flat, then every other number she could possibly think of, in the vain hope of finding Alex before Eastwich's new boss descended on them.

'Too late, *ma petite*,' Simon announced with satisfaction as Colin Mathieson, the senior production executive, appeared at the glass door of their office. He gave a brief courtesy knock before entering. A stranger who had to be the American followed him.

He wasn't at all what Tory had expected. She'd been prepared for a sharp-suited, forty something year old with a sun-bed tan and a roving eye.

That was why she stared. Well, that was what she told herself later. At the time she just stared.

Tall. Very tall. Six feet two or three. Almost casual in khaki trousers and an open-necked shirt. Dark hair, straight and slicked back, and a long angular face. Blue eyes, a quite startling hue. A mouth slanted with either humour or cynicism. In short, the best-looking man Tory had ever seen in her life.

Tory had never felt it before, an instant overwhelming attraction. She wasn't ready for it. She was transfixed. She was reduced to gaping stupidity.

The newcomer met her gaze and smiled as if he knew. No doubt it happened all the time. No doubt, being God's gift, he was used to it.

Colin Mathieson introduced her, 'Tory Lloyd, Production Assistant,' and she recovered sufficiently to raise a hand to the one stretched out to her. 'Lucas Ryecart, the new chief executive of Eastwich.'

Her hand disappeared in the warm dry clasp of his. He towered above her. She fought a feeling of insignificance. She couldn't think of a sane, sensible thing to say.

'Tory's worked for us for about a year,' Colin continued. 'Shows great promise. Had quite an input to the documentary on single mothers you mentioned seeing.'

Lucas Ryecart nodded and, finally dropping Tory's hand, commented succinctly, 'Well-made programme, Miss Lloyd...or is it Mrs?'

'Miss,' Colin supplied at her silence.

The American smiled in acknowledgement. 'Though perhaps a shade too controversial in intention.'

It took Tory a moment to realise he was still talking about the documentary and another to understand the criticism, before she at last emerged from brainless-guppy mode to point out, 'It's a controversial subject.'

Lucas Ryecart looked surprised by the retaliation but not unduly put out. 'True, and the slant was certainly a departure from the usual socialist dogma. Scarcely sympathetic.'

'We had no bias.' Tory remained on the defensive.

'Of course not,' he appeared to placate her, then added, 'You just gave the mothers free speech and let them condemn themselves.'

'We let them preview it,' she claimed. 'None of them complained.'

'Too busy enjoying their five minutes' fame, I expect,' he drawled back.

His tone was more dry than accusing, and he smiled again.

Tory didn't smile back. She was struggling with a mixture of temper and guilt, because, of course, he was right.

The single mothers in question had been all too ready to talk and it hadn't taken much editing to make them sound at best ignorant, at worst uncaring. Away from the camera and the lights, they had merely seemed lonely and vulnerable.

Tory had realised the interviews had been neither fair nor particularly representative and had suggested Alex tone them down. But Alex had been in no mood to listen. His wife had just left him, taking their two young children, and single mothers hadn't been flavour of the month.

Lucas Ryecart caught her brooding expression and ran on, 'Never mind...Tory, is it?'

Tory nodded silently, wishing he'd stuck to Miss Lloyd. Or did he feel he had to be on first-name terms with someone before he put the boot in?

'Tory,' he repeated, 'in documentary television it's always difficult to judge where to draw the line. Interview the mass murderer and are you explaining or glorifying his crimes? Interview the victims' families and do you redress the balance or simply make television out of people's grief?'

'I would refuse to do either,' Tory stated unequivocally at this mini-lecture.

'Really?' He raised a dark, straight brow and looked at her as if he were now assessing her as trouble.

It was Simon who came to her rescue, though not intentionally. '*I* wouldn't. I'd do anything for a good story.'

Having been virtually ignored, Simon thought it time to draw attention to himself.

Ryecart's eyes switched from Tory to Simon and Colin Mathieson performed the introductions. 'This is Simon Dixon. Alex's number two.'

'Simon.' The American nodded.

'Mr Ryecart.' Simon smiled confidently. 'Or do you wish us to call you Lucas? Being American, you must find English formality so outmoded.'

Tory had to give credit where credit was due: Simon had nerve.

Lucas Ryecart, however, scarcely blinked as he replied smoothly, 'Mr Ryecart will do for now.'

Simon was left a little red-faced, muttering, 'Well, you're the boss.'

'Quite,' Ryecart agreed succinctly, but didn't labour the point as he offered a conciliatory smile and hand to Simon.

Simon—the creep—accepted both.

It was Colin Mathieson who directed at them, 'Do you know where we might find Alex? He isn't in his office.'

'He never is,' muttered Simon in an undertone designed to be just audible.

Tory shot him a silencing look before saying, 'I think he's checking out locations for a programme.'

'Which programme?' Colin enquired. 'The one on ward closures? I thought we'd abandoned it.'

'Um…no.' Tory decided to keep the lies general. 'It's something at the conception stage, about…' She paused for inspiration and flushed as she felt the American's eyes on her once more.

'Alcoholism and the effects on work performance,' Simon volunteered for her.

She could have been grateful. She wasn't. She understood it for what it was—a snide reference to Alex's drinking.

Colin didn't seem to pick up on it, but Tory wasn't so sure about Lucas Ryecart. His glance switched to the mocking smile on Simon's face, then back to hers. He read the suppressed anger that made her mouth a tight line, but refrained from comment.

'Well, get Alex to give me a bell when he gets in.' Colin turned towards the door, ready to continue the guided tour.

Ryecart lingered, his eyes resting on Tory. 'Have we met before?'

Tory frowned. Where could they have met? They were unlikely to move in the same social circles.

'No, I don't think so,' she replied at length.

He seemed unconvinced but then shrugged. 'It doesn't matter. We probably haven't. I'm sure I would have remembered you.'

He smiled a hundred-watt smile, just for her, and the word handsome didn't cover it.

Tory's heart did an odd sort of somersault thing.

'I—I…' Normally so articulate, she couldn't think of a thing to say.

It was at least better than saying anything foolish.

He smiled again, a flash of white in his tanned face, then he was gone.

Tory took a deep, steadying breath and sat back down on her chair. Men like that should carry around a Government Health Warning.

'''I'm sure I would have remembered you.''' Simon mimicked the American's words. 'My God, where does he get his lines? B movies from the thirties? Still, good news for you, ducks.'

'What?' Tory looked blank.

'Come on, darling—' Simon thought she was being purposely obtuse '—you and the big chief. Has he got the hots for you or what?'

'You're being ridiculous!' she snapped in reply.

'Am I?' Simon gave her a mocking smile. 'Talk about long, lingering looks. And not just from our transatlantic cousin. Me think the Ice Maiden melteth.'

Tory clenched her teeth at this attempt at humour and confined herself to a glare. It seemed wiser than protesting, especially when she *could* recall staring overlong at the American.

Of course it hadn't lasted, the impact of his looks. The moment he had talked—or patronised might be closer to the mark—she had recovered rapidly.

'Well, who's to blame you?' Simon ran on. 'He has at least

one irresistible quality: he's rich. As in hugely, obscenely, embarrassingly—'

'Shut up, Simon,' she cut in, exasperated. 'Even if I was interested in his money, which I'm not, he definitely isn't my type.'

'If you say so.' He was clearly unconvinced. 'Probably as well. Rumour has it that he's still carrying a torch for his wife.'

'Wife?' she echoed. 'He's married?'

'*Was,*' he corrected. 'Wife died in a car accident a few years ago. Collided with a tanker lorry. Seemingly, she was pregnant at the time.'

The details struck a chord with Tory, and her stomach hit the floor. She shook her head in denial. No, it couldn't be.

Or could it?

Lucas could shorten to Luc. He was American. He did work in the media, albeit a quite different area.

'Was he ever a foreign correspondent?'

She willed Simon to ridicule the idea.

Instead he looked at her in surprise. 'As a matter of fact, yes, my sources tell me he worked for Reuters in the Middle East for several years before marrying into money. I can't remember the name of the family but they've Fleet Street connections.'

The Wainwrights. Tory knew it, though she could scarcely believe it. He'd been married to Jessica Wainwright. Tory knew this because she'd almost married into the same family.

How had she not recognised him immediately? She'd seen a photograph. It had pride of place on the grand piano—Jessica radiant in white marrying her handsome war reporter. Of course, it had been taken more than a decade earlier.

'Do you know him from some place, then?' Simon didn't hide his curiosity.

Tory shook her head. Telling Simon would be like telling the world.

'I remember reading about him in a magazine.' She hoped to kill the subject dead.

*   *   *

'Where are you going?' he asked, watching her pick up her handbag and jacket.

'Lunch,' she snapped back.

'It's not noon yet,' he pointed out, suddenly the model employee.

'It's either that or stay and murder you,' Tory retorted darkly.

'In that case,' Simon did his best to look contrite, '*bon appetit*!'

It deflated some of Tory's anger, but she still departed, needing fresh air and her own company. She made for the back staircase, expecting to meet no one on it. Most people used the lift.

Taking the stairs two at a time, she cannoned right into a motionless figure on the landing, bounced back off and, with a quick, 'Sorry,' would have kept on moving if a hand hadn't detained her. She looked up to find Lucas Ryecart staring down at her. Two meetings in half an hour was too much!

The American, however, didn't seem to think so. His face creased into a smile, transforming hard lines into undeniable charm. 'We meet again...*Tory*, isn't it?'

'I—I...yes.' Tory was reduced to monosyllables once more.

'Is everything all right?' He noted her agitation. He could hardly miss it. She must resemble a nervous rabbit caught in headlights.

She gathered her wits together, fast. 'Yes. Fine. I'm just going to the...dentist,' she lied unnecessarily. She could have easily said she was going to do some research.

'Well, at least it's not me,' he drawled in response.

Tory blinked. 'What's not?'

'Giving you that mildly terrified look,' he explained and slanted her a slow, amused smile.

Tory's brain went to mush again. 'I...no.'

'Check-up, filling or extraction?'

'Extraction.'

Tory decided an extraction might account for her flaky behaviour.

'I'll be back later,' she added, feeling like a naughty schoolgirl.

'Don't bother,' Lucas Ryecart dismissed. 'I'm sure Colin won't mind if you take the rest of the day off.'

He said this as Colin Mathieson appeared on the stairwell, holding up a file. 'Sorry I was so long, but it took some finding.'

'Good…Colin, Tory has to go to the dentist.' The American made a show of consulting him. 'Do you think we could manage without her this afternoon?'

Colin recognised the question for what it was—a token gesture. Lucas Ryecart called the shots now.

'Certainly, if she's under the weather,' Colin conceded, but he wasn't happy about it.

There were deadlines to be met and Alex was seldom around these days to meet them. Colin was well aware Tory and Simon were taking up the slack.

'I'll come in tomorrow,' she assured him quietly.

He gave her a grateful smile.

'Tory is a real workaholic,' he claimed, catching the frown settling between Lucas Ryecart's dark brows.

'Well, better than the other variety, I guess.' The American's eyes rested on Tory. He had a very direct, intense way of looking at a person.

Tory felt herself blush again. Could he possibly know why they were covering for Alex?

'I have to go.' She didn't wait for permission but took to her heels, flying down the stairs to exit Eastwich's impressive glass façade.

Having no dental appointment, she went straight back to her flat to hide out. It was on the ground floor of a large Victorian house on the outskirts of Norwich. She'd decided to rent rather than buy, as any career move would dictate a physical move. Maybe it would be sooner rather than later now Lucas Ryecart had descended on Eastwich.

Tory took out an album of old photographs and found one from five years ago. She felt relief, sure she'd changed almost out of recognition, her face thinner, her hair shorter, and her make-up considerably more sophisticated. She was no longer that dreamy-eyed girl who'd thought herself in love with Charlie Wainwright.

Coupled with a different name—Charlie had always preferred Victoria or Vicki to the Tory friends had called her—it was not surprising Lucas Ryecart had failed to make the connection. Chances were that all he'd seen of her was a snapshot, leaving the vaguest of memories, and all he'd heard was about a girl called Vicki who was at college with Charlie. Nobody special. A nice ordinary girl.

She could imagine Charlie's elegant mother using those exact words. Then, afterwards, Vicki had probably undergone a personality change from ordinary to common, and from nice to not very nice at all. What else, when the girl had broken her son's heart?

It was what Charlie had claimed at the time. Forget the fact that it had been his decision to end the engagement.

She took out another photograph, this one of Charlie's handsome, boyish face. She didn't know why she kept it. If she'd ever loved him, she certainly didn't now. It had all gone. Not even pain left.

Life had moved on. Charlie had the family he'd wanted and she had her career. She still had the occasional relationship but strictly on her terms with her in control.

She pulled a slight face. Well, normally. But where had been that control when she'd met Lucas Ryecart that morning? Lagging way behind the rest of her, that was where.

It had been like a scent, bypassing the brain and going straight for the senses. For a few moments it had been almost overpowering, as if she were drowning and had forgotten how to swim.

It hadn't lasted, of course. She'd surfaced pretty damn quickly when he'd begun to talk. She still bristled at his criticism on the single mothers documentary, regardless of whether it might be fair, and regardless of the fact that he'd bought Eastwich and along with it the right to express such opinions. She just had to recall what he'd said in that deep American drawl and she should be safe enough.

The question floated into her head. 'Safe from what?'

Tory, however, resolutely ignored it. Some things were better left well alone.

CHAPTER TWO

BY MORNING Tory had rationalised away any threat presented by Lucas Ryecart.

It could have been a simple chat-up line when he'd asked if they'd met before. Even if he'd seen a photograph of her, it would have left only the vaguest of impressions. And why should he make the connection between a girl student named Vicki and the Tory Lloyd who worked for him? She hadn't between Luc and Lucas until Simon had talked about his past and no one in Eastwich really knew about hers.

No, chances were he'd already forgotten her. He'd be like all the other chief executives before him—remote and faceless to someone in her junior position.

Reassured, Tory did as promised and went in to work, dressed casually in white T-shirt and cotton chinos. As it was Saturday, there were no calls to answer and, within an hour, she had dealt with most outstanding correspondence on her desk. The rest she took down the corridor for her boss's personal attention.

She didn't expect to find Alex Simpson there, not on a Saturday, and was initially pleased when she did. She imagined he'd come in to catch up on his own work.

That was before she noticed his appearance. There was several days' growth of beard on his chin and his eyes were bleary with sleep. His clothes were equally dishevelled and a quilt was draped along what he called his 'thinking' sofa, transforming it into a bed.

At thirty Alex Simpson had been hailed as a dynamic young programme-maker, destined for the highest awards. He had gone on to win several. Now he was pushing forty and, somewhere along the way, he had lost it.

'It's not how it looks.' He grimaced but was obviously relieved it was Tory and no one else. 'It's just that Sue's husband is home on leave and I've had no time to make other arrangements.'

Tory held in a sigh but she couldn't do anything about the disapproving look on her face. Officially Alex was lodging with Sue Baxter, a secretary at Eastwich, while he fixed himself up with more permanent accommodation. Unofficially he was sleeping with her while her Naval Engineer husband was on tour of duty. Tory knew this because *in*discretion was Sue Baxter's middle name.

She was a shallow, slightly vacuous woman, and what attraction Sue held for Alex was hard to fathom, but Tory kept her opinion to herself. Alex seemed intent on pushing his own self-destruct button and Tory felt ill-qualified to prevent him.

'You won't say anything, will you?' He smiled a little boyishly at Tory, already knowing the answer.

She shook her head, her loyalty guaranteed. She didn't fancy Alex, though many women did. Nor was she sure if she liked him at times. But he had a vulnerable quality that brought out a protective streak in her.

'You'd better not hang round here, looking like that,' she said with some frankness.

'I suppose not.' Alex made another face. 'I hear the new chief exec appeared in person yesterday.'

Tory nodded. 'I said you were out researching a programme.'

'I was, sort of,' he claimed. It was as unconvincing as his rider of, 'Pity I missed him.'

Tory looked at him sceptically, but refrained from pointing out that, had Lucas Ryecart met Alex while he was in this condition, Alex might not still be on the Eastwich payroll.

'Tory, I was wondering—' he gave her an appealing look '—if I could go to your place. Just to clean up. And maybe get my head down for an hour or two.'

Tory's heart sank. She told herself to refuse point-blank, but it came out as a less definite, 'I'm not sure, Alex. You know how tongues wag round here and if anyone saw you—'

'They won't,' he promised. ' I'll be the soul of discretion.'

'Yes, but—' Tory didn't get the chance to finish before Alex smiled in gratitude at her.

'You're a great girl.' He jumped up from his desk with some of his old enthusiasm. 'A wash and brush-up, that's all I need, and I'll be a new man.'

'All right.' Tory was already regretting it as she relayed, 'I have a spare key in my desk.'

Alex picked up the quilt from the couch and stuffed it into a cupboard, before following her back down the corridor to her office.

'You'll need the address.' She wrote it down on her telephone pad. 'You can use the phone to find a hotel or something.'

'Kind of you, Tory darling—' he looked rueful '—but I'm afraid hotels are out till pay day. My credit rating is zero and the bank is refusing to increase my overdraft.'

'What will you do? You can't keep dossing down in the office,' Tory warned.

'No, you're right. I don't suppose you could...' he began hopefully, then answered for himself, 'No, forget it. I'll find somewhere.'

Tory realised what he'd been about to ask. She also understood he was still asking, by not asking. His eyes were focused on her like a homeless stray.

She tried to harden her heart. She reminded herself that Alex earned a great deal more than her for doing a great deal less. Was it her problem that he couldn't manage his money?

'Never mind.' He forced a brave smile. 'I'll be back on my feet soon. I'm due my annual bonus from Eastwich next month—that's assuming this American chappie doesn't cancel it.'

Or cancel him, Tory thought as she looked at Alex through Lucas Ryecart's eyes. He was a shambolic figure whose past awards would be just history.

'Look, you can use my couch,' Tory found herself offering, 'until pay-day.'

'Darling Tory, you're a life-saver.' A delighted Alex made to give her a hug but she fended him off.

'And strictly on a keep-your-hands-to-yourself basis,' she added bluntly.

'Of course.' Alex took a step from her and held up his hands in compliance. 'No problem. I know you're not interested.'

He should do. Tory had made it clear enough in the beginning and Alex, philanderer though he undoubtedly was, respected the fact. He was also lazy; mostly he ended up with women who chased him. Being handsome in a slightly effete way, he drew a certain type of woman. Tory wasn't included in their category.

'Five days.' Tory calculated when their next salary should appear in the bank.

'Fine.' Alex gave her another grateful smile before turning to go.

'Alex,' Tory called him back at the door, 'try and stay sober, please.'

For a moment Alex looked resentful, ready to protest his innocence. Tory's expression stopped him. It wasn't critical or superior or contemptuous. It was simply appealing.

He nodded, then, acknowledging his growing problem, said, 'If I don't, I'll crash somewhere else. Okay?'

'Okay.' Tory hoped his promise was sincere. He wasn't a violent drunk but she still didn't want him round her place in that state.

After Alex had gone, she wondered just how big a mistake she'd made. She knew it was one. She trusted it would turn out to be of the minor variety.

Rather than dwell on it, she returned to her work, but was interrupted minutes later. Her door opened and she looked up, expecting to see Alex again. She stared wordlessly at the man in the doorway.

Overnight she'd decided it was a passing attraction she'd felt towards Lucas Ryecart. Only it hadn't yet. Passed, that was. Dressed in black jeans, white shirt and dark glasses, he was just as devastating.

'How's the tooth?' he asked.

'The tooth?' she repeated stupidly.

'Gone but not forgotten?' he suggested.

The tooth. Tory clicked. She'd have to acquire a better memory if she were going to take up lying to this man.

'It's fine,' she assured. 'Actually, I had forgotten all about it.'

'Good.' His eyes ran over her, making her feel her T-shirt outlined her body too clearly. 'You didn't have to come in. How do you usually spend your Saturdays?'

The same way, Tory could have admitted, but somehow she didn't think he'd be impressed, even if he now owned most of Eastwich. More like he'd think she had nothing better to do with her time.

'It varies.' She shrugged noncommittally, then glanced down at her work, as if anxious to get on with it.

He noted the gesture, and switched to asking, 'Has Simpson gone?'

'Simpson?' Tory stalled.

'Alex Simpson.' He leaned on the doorframe, eyes inscrutable behind the dark glasses. 'At least I assume it was Simpson and not some passing bum, making himself at home in his office.'

'Alex was here, yes,' she confirmed and went on inventively, 'He came in to catch up on his paperwork.'

'He was catching up on some sleep when I saw him,' countered Ryecart.

'Really?' Tory faked surprise quite well. 'He did say he'd been in very early. Perhaps he nodded off without realising.'

'Slept it off, is my guess,' the American drawled back, and, pushing away from the door, crossed to sit on the edge of her desk. He removed the glasses and appraised her for a moment or two before adding, 'Are you two an item? Is that it?'

'An item?' Tory was slow on the uptake.

'You and Simpson, are you romantically involved?' He spelt out his meaning.

'No, of course not!' Tory denied most vehemently.

It had little impact, as the American smiled at her flash of temper. 'No need go nuclear. I was only asking. I hear Simpson has something of a reputation with women,' he remarked, getting Tory's back up further.

'And from that you concluded that he and I…that we are…'
She was unwilling to put it into words.

He did it for her. 'Lovers?'

Tory found herself blushing. He had that effect.

He studied her, as if she were an interesting species, and
her blush deepened. 'I didn't think women did that any more.'

'Possibly not the women you know,' Tory shot back before
she could stop herself.

He understood the insult. He could easily have sacked her
for it. Instead he laughed.

'True,' he conceded. 'I tend to prefer the more experienced
kind. Less hassle. Lower expectations. And fewer recriminations at the end… Still, who knows? I could be reformed.'

And pigs might fly, Tory thought as she wondered if he was
flirting with her or just making fun.

'What about you?' he said with the same lazy smile.

'Me?' she asked. 'Oh, I prefer the invisible kind. Much less
hassle. Zero expectations. And absolutely no recriminations.'

It took the American an instant to interpret. 'You don't
date?'

'I don't date,' Tory repeated but without his tone of disbelief, 'and I don't need reforming, either.'

He looked puzzled rather than annoyed, his eyes doubting
her seriousness.

'Is that a targeted response,' he finally asked, 'or a general
declaration of intent?'

'Come again?' Tory squinted at him.

'Are you just telling *me* to take a hike,' he translated, 'or
are all men off the agenda?'

Tory debated how much she wanted to keep her job. Just
enough to show some restraint, she decided, so she said nothing. Her eyes, however, said much more.

'Me, I guess,' he concluded with a confidence barely dented.
'Well, never mind, I can live in hope.'

He was laughing at her. He had to be. He wasn't really
interested in her. It was all a joke to him.

He straightened from the edge of her desk, saying, 'Would
you have some idea how I might contact Simpson? '

'I…I'm not sure.' Having denied any relationship with Alex, Tory could hardly reveal the fact he was holed up at her place. 'I might be able to get a message to him.'

'Fine. I've asked all senior department heads to meet me, nine a.m. Monday, for a briefing,' he explained. 'It would be advisable for Simpson to attend.'

Tory nodded. 'I'll tell him…I mean, if I get hold of him,' she qualified, anxious to dispel the notion she and Alex had anything other than a business relationship.

'Well, if you can't, don't worry about it,' he ran on. 'It's Simpson's problem if he can't give Personnel a current telephone number.'

Tory frowned. 'But you saw him this morning.'

'So why didn't I wake him up?' he asked the question that was clearly in her mind. 'Let's just say I thought the morning after wouldn't be the best time to meet a new boss. What do you think?'

Tory thought that remarkably fair of the American—to give Alex the chance to redeem himself. Of course, he might simply prefer to sack him when he was stone-cold sober.

'Alex is a very good programme-maker,' she declared staunchly. 'He won a BAFTA three years ago.'

'Simpson *was* a very good programme-maker,' Lucas Ryecart corrected her, 'and, in this business, you're only as good as your last show. Simpson should know that.'

Tory said nothing. Speaking up for Alex had cut no ice with this man.

He also suspected her motives. 'Why so concerned about Simpson? If he goes, it might do your own career some good.'

'I doubt it.' Tory wondered who he was trying to fool. 'Simon is more experienced than me.'

He frowned, making the connection only when she glanced towards the second desk in the room. 'More willing to promote his cause, too, as I recall. Is he the reason you're loyal to Simpson?'

'Sorry?'

'You don't want to work for this Simon guy?'

No, Tory certainly didn't, but she didn't want to do Simon down either.

'You're not homophobic, are you?' he surmised at her uneasy silence.

'What?' Tory was startled by his directness.

'Homophobic,' he repeated, 'Anti-gay, against homo—'

'I know what it means!' Tory cut in angrily, and, forgetting—or, at least, no longer caring—who he was, informed him, 'It might be hard for an American to understand, but reticence isn't always an indication of stupidity.'

'Being brash, loud-mouth colonials, you mean.' He had no problem deciphering the insult. He just wasn't bothered by it.

Tory wondered what you had to do to dent this man's confidence. Use a sledgehammer, perhaps.

'Simon's sexual preference is a matter of complete disinterest to me,' she declared in heavy tones.

'If you say so,' he responded, as if he didn't quite believe her.

'I am *not* homophobic!' she insisted angrily. 'Whether I'd want to work for Simon doesn't hinge on that.'

'Okay.' He conceded the point, then immediately lost interest in it as he looked at his watch, saying, 'I have to go. I have a meeting in London. I'll give you my number.'

He picked up her Biro and, tearing out a slip of paper from her notepad, leaned on her desk to write his name and two telephone numbers.

'The top one is my mobile,' he informed her. 'The other's Abbey Lodge. I'm staying there in the short term.'

Abbey Lodge was the most exclusive hotel locally, favoured by high-powered businessmen and visiting celebrities.

He held out the piece of paper and for a moment Tory just stared at it as if it were contaminated. Why was he giving her his telephone number? Did he imagine she'd want to call him?

'In case you have a problem tracking down Alex Simpson,' he explained, patently amused at her wary expression.

'Of course.' Now she almost snatched the paper from him.

'Still, if you want to call me, regardless—' his mouth

slanted '—feel free. I'm sure we can find *something* to talk about…'

'I…' On the contrary Tory couldn't think of a sensible thing to say. She'd been so presumptuous it was embarrassing.

'Meanwhile—' his smile became less mocking '—it's a beautiful day. Why not play hooky for once?'

The suggestion sounded genuine but Tory felt even more uncomfortable, recalling the fact she'd played hooky yesterday.

'I have some stuff to finish,' she claimed, sober-faced.

'Well, you know what they say: all work and no play,' he misquoted dryly, 'makes for a dull television producer.'

Tory realised he was joking but wondered, nonetheless, if that was how she seemed to him. Dull. What an indictment.

It put her on the defensive. 'I'm not the one travelling down to London for a business meeting on a Saturday.'

'Did I say business?' He raised a dark brow.

Tory frowned up at him. He had, hadn't he?

He shook his head, adding, 'No, this one's strictly personal.'

'I'm sorry.' Tory denied any intention to pry.

But he continued, 'In a way, it involves you. I'm having dinner with the woman I was dating until recently…a *farewell* dinner,' he stressed.

Tory met his eyes briefly, then looked away once more. There was nothing subtle about his interest in her.

'This really is none of my business, Mr Ryecart,' she replied on an officious note.

'Not now, maybe—' he got to his feet '—but who knows what the future might hold?'

He afforded her another smile. Perfect white teeth in a tanned face. Too handsome for anyone else's good.

Tory tried again. 'I shouldn't think we'll meet very often, Mr Ryecart,' she said repressively, 'in view of your considerably senior position, but I'm sure I'll endeavour to be polite when we do.'

This time her message couldn't be missed. 'In short, you'd like me to take a hike.'

Tory's nails curled into her palms. The man had no idea of the conventions that governed normal conversation.

'I didn't say that,' she replied, through gritted teeth. 'I was just pointing out—'

'That you'd touch your forelock but nothing else,' he summed up with breath-taking accuracy.

Tory felt a curious desire to hit him. It took a huge effort to stop herself, to remind herself he *was* her boss.

He held up a pacifying hand, having clearly read her thoughts. He might be brash, but he wasn't stupid.

'Tell you what, let's agree to dispense with the forelock-tugging, too,' he suggested and finally walked towards the door.

Tory's heart sank. What did that mean?

'Mr Ryecart—' she called after him.

He turned, his expression now remote. Had he already dispensed with her, altogether?

She didn't intend waiting to find out. She asked point-blank, 'Should I be looking for another job?'

'What?' Such an idea had obviously been far from his mind. He considered it briefly before answering, 'If you're asking me will Eastwich survive, then I don't know that yet. It's no secret that it's operating at a loss, but I wouldn't have bought it if I didn't feel turn-around was viable.'

It was a straight, businesslike response that left Tory feeling decidedly silly. She had imagined rejecting Lucas Ryecart might be a sackable offence but obviously he didn't work that way.

'That isn't what you meant, is it?' He read her changing expression.

'No,' Tory admitted reluctantly. 'I thought...'

'That I'd fire you for not responding to my advances,' he concluded for himself, and now displeasure thinned his sensual mouth. 'God, you have a low opinion of me...or is it all men?'

Tory bit on her lip before muttering, 'I—I...if I misjudged you—'

'In spades,' he confirmed. 'I may be the loud, overbearing American you've already written me off as—'

'That's not—' Tory tried to deny it.

He overrode her. 'And I may let what's in my pants overrule good sense occasionally,' he continued crudely, 'but desperate I'm not, or vindictive. If you leave Eastwich, it won't be on my account.'

Tory wanted the ground to swallow her up. She started to say, 'I'm sorry, I shouldn't have—' and was left talking to thin air.

Lucas Ryecart might not be vindictive but he had a temper. She experienced its full force as the door slammed hard behind him.

And that's me told, she thought, feeling wrung out and foolish, and wishing she'd kept her mouth shut.

He'd been flirting with her. Nothing more. Perhaps he flirted with all personable women under the assumption that most would enjoy it. He'd be right, too. Most would.

They'd know how to take Lucas Ryecart, realise that anyone that handsome, and rich, and successful, would scarcely be interested in ordinary mortals. They'd be slightly flattered by his appreciative gaze, a little charmed by his slow, easy smile, but they certainly wouldn't be crazy enough to take him seriously.

She glanced out of the window in time to see him striding across the car park. She didn't worry that he'd look up. She was already forgotten.

She watched him get into a dark green four-by-four. It was a surprisingly *un*flash vehicle. She'd have expected him to drive something fast and conspicuous—a low-slung sports car, perhaps. But what did she really know about Lucas Ryecart? Next to nothing.

She tried to remember what Charlie, her ex-fiancé, had said. He hadn't talked much of his dead sister but he'd mentioned her husband a few times. He'd obviously admired the older man who'd spent his early career reporting from the trouble spots of the world. Charlie's mother had also alluded to her American son-in-law with some fondness and Tory had formed various images: faithful husband, dedicated journalist, fine human being.

None fitted the Lucas Ryecart she'd met, but then it had been years since Jessica Wainwright's death and time changed everybody. It had certainly changed his circumstances if Eastwich was only one of the television companies he owned. He was also no longer the marrying kind, a fact he'd made clear. Arguably, his directness was a virtue, but if he had any other noble character traits Tory had missed them.

Time had changed Tory, too. Or was it her current lifestyle? All work and no play, as he'd said. Making her dull, stupid even, unable to laugh off a man's interest without sounding like prude of the year.

Tory felt like kicking herself. And Alex. And Lucas Ryecart. She settled for kicking her waste bin and didn't hang around to tidy up the mess she made.

She took the American's advice and spent the afternoon at the Anglian Country Club, a favourite haunt for young professionals. For two hours she windsurfed across the man-made lake, a skill she'd acquired on her first foreign holiday. It was her main form of relaxation, strenuous though it could be, and she was now more than competent.

Sometimes she took a lesson with Steve, the resident coach. About her age, he had a law degree but had never practised, preferring to spend his life windsurfing. They had chatted occasionally and once gone for a drink in the club but nothing more. Today he helped her put away her equipment and asked casually if she had plans for the evening. She shook her head and he proposed going for something to eat in town.

Normally Tory would have politely turned him down, but Lucas Ryecart's image loomed, and she said, 'Why not?'

Tory drove them in her car and they went to an Italian restaurant. They talked about windsurfing, then music and the colleges they'd attended. Steve was easy enough company.

They went on to a pub and met some of his friends, a mixed crowd of men and women. Tory stuck to orange juice, and, although declining a party invitation, agreed to drive them there.

When the rest had piled out of her car, Steve surprised her with a kiss on the lips. It was quite pleasurable, but hardly earth-moving and another man's image intruded when she closed her eyes. She broke off the kiss before it turned intimate.

Steve got the message. 'I don't suppose you'd like to go home to my place?' he asked, more in hope than expectation.

'No, thanks all the same.' She gave him an amiable smile and her refusal was accepted in the same spirit.

Steve bowed out with a casual, 'Perhaps we can go out again some time,' and followed his friends into the house where the party was.

Tory drove home without regrets. She'd enjoyed the evening up to a point, but she had no desire to have competent, athletic sex with a man whose *raison d'être* was windsurfing. She'd sooner go to bed with a mug of Horlicks and a Jane Austen.

She returned to find her flat empty and felt a measure of relief, assuming Alex had chosen somewhere else to doss down.

No such luck, however, as she was rudely awakened at two in the morning by a constant ringing on her doorbell. Pulling on a dressing gown, she went to the bay window first and wasn't entirely surprised to see Alex leaning against the wall.

'Lost my key, sorry,' he slurred as she opened the outer door and took in his swaying figure.

'Oh, Alex, you promised.' She sighed wearily and for a moment contemplated shutting the door on him.

'Couldn't help it,' he mumbled pathetically. 'Love her, really love her... Know that, Tory?'

'Yes, Alex. Now, shh!' Tory hastily propelled him through the hallway before he woke her neighbours.

'I'm not drunk.' He breathed whisky fumes on her as he lurched inside her flat. 'Just had a drink or two. Her fault. The bitch. Phoned her up but she wouldn't talk to me.'

Tory sighed again as he sprawled his length on her sofa. There would be no moving him now. She should have turned him away.

'Why won't she talk to me?' he appealed with an injured air. 'She knows she's the only one I've ever loved.'

'Her husband was probably there,' Tory pointed out in cynical tones.

'Husband?' He turned bleary eyes towards her, then rallied to claim belligerently, 'I'm her husband. Eyes of God and all that. Better or worse. Richer or poorer. Till death or the mortgage company do us part,' he finished on a self-pitying sob.

'Who are we talking about, Alex?' Tory finally asked.

'Rita, of course.' A frown questioned her intelligence, then he began to sing, 'Lovely Rita, no one can beat her—'

'Shh!' Tory hushed him once more. 'You're going to wake the woman upstairs.'

'Don't care,' Alex announced, this time like a sulky boy. 'All women are vile... 'Cept you, darling Tory.' He smiled winningly at her.

Tory rolled her eyes heavenward. She might have taken Lucas Ryecart too seriously that morning, but she was in no danger of it with Alex. Drunk, Alex would flirt with a lamppost.

'I thought you were talking about Sue,' she stated in repressive tones.

'Sue?' He looked blank for a moment.

'Sue Baxter,' she reminded him heavily. 'Works at Eastwich. Husband in Navy. Woman you've been living with for the last month or two.'

Drunk though he was, Alex understood the implication. 'You think I don't love Rita because I've been shacking up with Sue? But I do. Sue's just...'

'A fill-in?' Tory suggested dryly.

'Yes. No. You don't understand,' he answered in quick succession. 'Men aren't the same as women, Tory, you have to realise that.'

'Oh, I do,' Tory assured him, and before he could justify his infidelity on biological grounds she stood and picked up the blanket and pillow she'd dug out earlier. 'You're an education in yourself, Alex,' she added, draping the blanket over him without ceremony. 'Lift.'

He raised his head and she thrust the pillow under him.

'You're not a woman, Tory,' he told her solemnly, 'you're a friend.'

'Thanks,' she muttered at this backhanded compliment. Not that she minded much. She didn't want Alex's roving eye fixing on her. 'Goodnight, Alex.'

''Night, Tory,' he echoed, already settling down for the night. Soon he would be out for the count.

It was Tory who was left sleepless.

After an afternoon spent windsurfing and an evening in company, she should be tired enough to sleep through a hurricane, yet she couldn't sleep through Lucas Ryecart.

Alex had provided a temporary distraction but now he was just another concern. How could she keep Alex sober tomorrow so he would be presentable on Monday for his meeting with Ryecart?

She tried telling herself it wasn't her problem. And it wasn't, really. After all, what did she owe Alex? He had given her a chance, taking her on as a production assistant when she'd had little experience, but she'd surely repaid him, covering up for him as she had over that last three months. It would be much the wisest thing to let Alex fend for himself.

Perhaps Alex might even hold his own with the American. After all, he was an intelligent, articulate man with a first-class degree from Cambridge and twenty years' experience in the television industry.

Whereas Lucas Ryecart, who was he?

The man who was going to wipe the floor with Alex, that was who, she answered the question for herself, and for the second night in a row fell asleep with Lucas Ryecart's image running round her brain.

CHAPTER THREE

TORY woke in an extremely bad mood, and felt not much better after taking a shower. Dressed in jeans and T-shirt, she went through to the living room to tackle Alex. She had decided: she wanted him gone, a.s.a.p.

Only he wasn't awake yet. With his arms tight round a cushion and his legs bent up on the sofa, he lay there muttering in his sleep. He looked a wreck and he smelled awful, of too much booze and nicotine. She'd never found Alex attractive; this morning he was positively repellent. No way was he going to get his act together by Monday.

But she realised that she wouldn't need to give him a hard time. When Alex woke up, he would feel sorry enough for himself.

She was right. When she woke him with strong black coffee, he was full of remorse.

He'd forgotten his promise not to return to her flat drunk. Apparently he'd had a whisky for Dutch courage before phoning his wife in Edinburgh. When she'd slammed the phone down on him, he'd had several more.

'So, basically it was all Rita's fault,' Tory concluded on a sceptical note, deciding a sympathetic approach wasn't going to help him.

He looked a little sheepish. 'I didn't say that, exactly.'

'Just as well,' Tory muttered back, 'because I haven't met many candidates for living sainthood, but your wife has to be one.'

He looked taken aback by her frankness, but didn't argue. 'You're right. I didn't treat her very well, did I?'

Tory's brows went heavenward.

'Okay, I admit it,' he groaned back. 'I was unfaithful to her

32

a couple of times, but it didn't mean anything. It's Rita I love. After twenty years together she should know that.'

'*Twenty years?*' Tory hadn't viewed Alex as long-term married.

'We met at college,' Alex went on. 'She was so bright and funny and together. She still is... If only I'd realised. I can't function without Rita,' he claimed in despair.

'Then you'd better try and get her back,' Tory advised quite severely. 'Either that, or get your own act together, Alex, before you lose it all.'

'I already have,' he said miserably.

Tory resisted the urge to shake him. 'Hardly. You have an exceedingly well-paid job doing something you used to love. Give it another week or so, however, and you'll probably be kissing goodbye to that, too.'

Alex looked a little shocked at her plain-speaking, then resentful. 'It's not that bad. Sure, I've missed a few deadlines and been absent for a meeting or two. But Colin understands. He knows I'll be back on track soon.'

'You've forgotten the American.' Tory hadn't.

'Ryecart.' Alex shrugged at the name. 'So, there's a new chief exec. He'll only be interested in the business side.'

'I don't think so.' Tory decided not to pass on Ryecart's comments about their last documentary but decided Alex still required a reality check. 'There's something you should know. He saw you yesterday morning, crashed on your office couch.'

'Damn,' Alex cursed aloud, before saying with some hope, 'Maybe he thought I'd been working all night.'

Tory shook her head again. 'This man's not stupid, Alex. He knew you were sleeping it off... He wants to see you first thing Monday morning.'

'Well, isn't that civilised of him,' Alex sneered, 'not waking a sleeping man? Making me sweat till Monday morning before sacking me.'

That scenario had already occurred to Tory, but she said nothing.

'He was probably too much a coward to do it on Saturday,' Alex ran on speculatively. 'Probably thought I'd turn round and punch his lights out for him.'

Tory sighed heavily. 'Men are ridiculous.'

That deflated Alex somewhat. They both knew he was as likely to punch someone as become celibate.

'All right, so I'm no fighter, but he wouldn't know that.'

'I doubt he'd care. He looks well able to take care of himself.'

'Big?' Alex deduced from her tone.

'Huge.' Tory reckoned the American was at least six inches taller than Alex.

'Upwards or outwards?'

'Both… Well, sort of. He's not fat. He's just…muscly, you might say,' Tory described him with some reluctance.

Alex slanted her a curious look. 'You don't fancy him, do you, Tory?'

'No, of course not!' she protested immediately. 'Whatever makes you say that?'

He shrugged, then smiled a fraction. 'The blush on your face, I suppose. I've never seen you blush before.'

'Rubbish. I'm always blushing. I'm like a Belisha beacon in hot weather,' she declared extravagantly and turned the conversation back on him. 'Anyway, we're not talking about me. It's you that has the problem. You're going to have to make an effort on Monday, Alex, to impress him.'

'Is there any point?' he asked rhetorically. 'Why go in and give him the satisfaction of firing me?'

'Oh, for God's sake, Alex!' She lost her patience. 'Stop being such a wimp!'

For a moment Alex looked seriously indignant. He was her boss, after all. Then he remembered he'd just spent the night sleeping on her sofa, and had pretty much surrendered his right to deference by offloading his problems on her.

'I'm sorry. I shouldn't have said that,' Tory added as his face caved in, exposing his vulnerability.

'No, it's all right. It's what Rita would have said to me. She couldn't stand people wallowing in self-pity.' He looked in admiration at Tory, and her heart sank. She didn't need Alex transferring his emotional dependence onto her.

'Well, it's up to you, Alex. I'm not going to tell you what

to do.' She rose abruptly to collect their coffee-cups and take them through to the small kitchen adjoining.

He followed her and watched as she rinsed them out in the sink. 'I could prepare a schedule of documentaries we propose to make in the coming months.'

Tory frowned. 'What documentaries?'

He shrugged. 'I'm sure we could come up with something.'

'We?' she echoed.

'I thought, well, that you might—'

'Give up my *one* day off?'

'Well, if you've plans...' He clearly believed she hadn't.

'You think my life is dull, too, don't you?' she accused, almost wiping the pattern off the saucer she was drying. 'Good old Tory, with nothing better to do at the weekend.'

'No, of course not,' Alex disclaimed quickly, realising he'd touched a sore spot.

Tory scowled, but not at him. It was Lucas Ryecart's comments that still rankled. She couldn't seem to get the man out of her head.

'I just know I'll work better with you as a sounding-board,' Alex added appeasingly.

Tory knew he wouldn't work *at all* if she didn't help him.

She gave in. 'You go wash, I'll make the coffee, then we'll get started.'

'Tory, you're a brick.'

Tory pulled a face as he went from the kitchen to the hall and the bathroom off it. She heard the shower running shortly afterwards and, above it, the sound of him singing. She pulled another face. What did he have to sing about?

Men were unbelievable. One moment Alex was confessing his undying love for his wife and his devastation at her loss, the next he was singing a selection of top-twenty hits from the seventies.

Compartmentalisation. That was the key to the male psyche. Everything kept in separate little cubicles. Love of wife and children. Work and ambition. Fun and sex. Duty and religion. Nip into one cubicle, pull the curtain and forget the rest. Then nip out and onto the next. Never mind tidying up what you've left behind on the floor.

Not all men, of course, but the majority. She thought of Lucas Ryecart. Another compartmentaliser. One moment she was a woman and he was making it damn plain he fancied her. The next she was one of his employees and he clearly had no problems treating her as such. Then he was gone, and no doubt she'd been forgotten the second he'd climbed into his car.

So very different from women. Women stood at windows, watching cars pull away while they sorted out what they felt and why. Women carried their emotional baggage between cubicles until they were bowed with the weight.

There were exceptions, of course. Her own mother was one. Maura Lloyd had a simple approach to life. Create what havoc you liked, then shut the door on it and move on. It had worked for her—if not for the people round her.

Tory had been Maura's only child. She'd had her at eighteen. Tory's father had been a married lecturer at art college. At least that was one of the stories Maura had told her, but at times he'd also been a famous painter, a cartoonist in a popular daily paper, and an illustrator for children's story-books. Tory was never sure whether these were total fantasy or a selection of different men who might have sired her or the same multi-talented many-careered individual. Whichever, Maura had consistently avoided naming the man throughout Tory's twenty-six years, and, having met some of Maura's later partners, Tory had decided to leave well alone.

At any rate, Maura had decided to keep her. After a fashion, anyway, as Tory had spent her childhood shuttling back and forth between gentle, unassuming grandparents who lived in a semi in the suburbs to various flats her mother had occupied with various men.

The contrast couldn't have been sharper, order versus chaos, routine versus excitement, respectability versus an extravagantly Bohemian lifestyle. Tory had never felt neglected, just torn and divided.

She loved her mother because she was warm and funny and

affectionate, but, in truth, she preferred living with her grand-parents. When she'd become sick as a child, her mother hadn't pretended to cope. Grandmother Jean had been the one to take her to chemotherapy and hold her hand and promise her her beautiful curls would grow back.

It wasn't that Maura hadn't cared. Tory didn't believe that. But it had been a selfish sort of caring. When Tory had needed calm, Maura would be playing the tragic figure, weeping so extravagantly a ten-year-old Tory had become hysterical, imagining she must be dying.

She hadn't died, of course, and the childhood leukaemia was now a distant memory, although, in some respects, it still shaped her life. She supposed everything in childhood did.

She looked round her kitchen—everything in its place and a place for everything. Grandmother Jean's influence, although she'd been dead ten years and her grandfather for longer.

There was no visible sign of her mother but Tory knew she carried some of her inside. She just kept it locked up tight.

'Tory?' A voice broke into her thoughts. 'Are you all right?'

'Sure. I've made coffee.' She loaded a tray with the cafetère and cups and a plate of croissants.

Alex followed her through and, after a slow start, they began to trawl up some ideas for future programmes.

They worked all day, with only the briefest break for a sand-wich lunch, and as Alex got into his stride the man who had won awards re-emerged. Tory remembered why she had wanted to work for him in the first place. When he wasn't bed-hopping or pub-crawling, Alex Simpson was a fairly talented programme-maker.

In the end they came up with four firm proposals for future programmes and a promising outline of another. Alex sat back, looking pleased with himself, as well he might, while Tory had some satisfaction in imagining Lucas Ryecart's reaction.

'Where's your nearest take-away?' Alex asked, consulting his watch to find it after six.

'There's a Chinese a couple of streets away,' she replied. 'I have a menu list somewhere. We can phone in an order, then I'll collect it.'

She went to a notice-board in the kitchen and found the menu list for the Lucky Dragon. They made their selection and she did the calling.

Alex followed her through to the hall, saying, 'I should go,' as he watched her sling on a lightweight jacket.

'You don't know where it is.' Tory slipped out the door before he could argue.

The Lucky Dragon was, in fact, easy to find. The problem was one had to pass The Brown Cow pub on the way, and Tory wasn't sure whether Alex would manage to *pass* it.

She went on foot and the food was ready by the time she arrived. She walked back quickly so it wouldn't go cold. She didn't notice the Range Rover parked on the other side of the street or its owner, crossing to trail her up the steps to her front door.

'I'll do that,' he offered just as she put the take-away on the doorstep so she could use her key.

Tory recognised the voice immediately and wheeled round.

Lucas Ryecart took a step back at her alarmed look. 'Sorry if I startled you.'

Tory felt a confusion of things. As usual, there was the physical impact of him, tall, muscular and utterly male. That caused a first rush of excitement, hastily suppressed, closely followed by the set-your-teeth-on-edge factor as she realised a series of things. He had her address. Her address was on a file. He had her file. He owned her file. He owned Eastwich.

He just didn't own her, Tory reminded both of them as a frown made it plain he wasn't welcome.

'I wanted to speak to you,' he pursued. 'I decided it might be better outside work hours… Can I come in?'

'I…no!' Tory was horrified by the idea. She wanted no one, especially not this particular one, to find out Alex was using her flat as a base.

'You have company?' he surmised.

'What makes you say that?' Her tone denied it.

He glanced down at the plastic bags from which the smell of food was emanating. 'Well, either that, or you have a very healthy appetite.'

Sherlock Holmes lives, Tory thought in irritation and lied quite happily. 'I have a friend round for tea.'

'And I'm intruding,' he concluded for himself. 'No problem, this won't take long. I just wanted to say sorry.'

'Sorry? For what?'

'Yesterday morning. I was way out of line. Wrong time, wrong place, and I was moving too fast.'

Tory was unsure how to react to what seemed a genuine apology.

'I—I…this really isn't necessary,' she finally replied. 'We both said things. I'd prefer just to forget the whole incident.'

'Fine. Let's shake on that.' He offered her his hand.

'Right.' Tory took it with some reservations.

His grip was firm and strong and it jolted her, as if his touch were electric. Warmth spread through her like a slow fire.

Quite alarming. To be turned on by a handshake. Even the thought brought a flush to her pale cheeks.

He noticed it and smiled. Did he know?

'You're very young,' he said, out of nowhere.

She shook her head. 'I'm twenty-six.'

'That's young.' He smiled without mockery. 'I'm forty-one.'

Tory's eyes widened, betraying her surprise. He didn't look it.

'Too old, I reckon,' he added, shaking his head.

'For what?' Tory asked rather naively.

'For girls young enough to be my daughter,' he concluded, laughing at himself now.

No, you're not. Tory almost said the words aloud. But why, when she wanted rid of him? Didn't she?

She looked down. They were still holding hands. She slipped from his grip. The warmth between them remained.

'Colin Mathieson told me you were in your thirties,' he recalled next.

Tory's heart sank a little. Colin *believed* she was in her thirties. It was a wrong impression fostered by Alex when he'd employed her for the job.

'Perhaps he was thinking of someone else,' Tory suggested weakly.

'Perhaps,' he echoed. 'Anyway, if I'd known your real age, I wouldn't have asked you out.'

It was Tory's turn to frown. Did he have some religious objection to women under thirty? Or did he imagine her too immature to interest him?

'You didn't,' she pointed out.

'Didn't I?' He arched a brow before admitting, 'Well, it had been my game plan. I guess I didn't get round to it.'

Now she was too young or inexperienced or whatever for him to bother, Tory surmised with some anger, surely irrational.

'It was Colin who gave me your address,' he went on. 'I told him I wanted to talk to you about Simpson.'

Alex? For a moment or two Tory had forgotten about Alex.

She could tell the American, of course. She could invite him in so he could meet a sober, industrious Alex. Did it matter if he jumped to the wrong conclusions about him being there?

Tory found it did matter, so she said nothing.

'Did you manage to locate him, by the way?' Lucas enquired directly.

She nodded.

'He's looking forward to meeting you,' she fabricated. 'I believe he has some future projects he wishes to discuss.'

Lucas Ryecart looked mildly surprised but didn't challenge it.

'Good.' He then began to say, 'I guess I'd better leave you to your meal—' when the door opened behind Tory.

She turned to see Alex and this time her heart plummeted. He was holding his jacket, obviously on his way out. On seeing her, his face clouded with guilt.

Tory was quick to realise where he'd been going. Tired of waiting for the meal, he'd been off in search of liquid refreshment.

'There you are.' Alex recovered quickly. 'I was worried you'd got lost and was coming to look for you.'

'No, I...' She glanced between the two men but made no effort to introduce them.

Lucas Ryecart, of course, knew exactly who Alex was. His eyes briefly registered the other man, then slid back to Tory and didn't leave her. Dark blue eyes, cold with anger.

'Sorry—' Alex picked up on the sudden drop in temperature '—I can see I'm in the way. Would you like me to disappear for an hour or two? Let you have the flat to yourself?'

Tory could have groaned aloud. Alex made it sound as if they were sharing the place.

'I...no, don't do that, Alex.' She'd spent all day getting his mind back on work. She wasn't giving him a chance to go AWOL on her.

It was the wrong answer as far as Lucas Ryecart was concerned.

'No, don't do that, *Alex*,' he mimicked her anxious tone, reading too much—far too much—into it. 'Miss Lloyd and I have finished any business between us for now.'

Having said his piece, he turned and walked away.

'Damn!' Tory swore in frustration.

Alex, having registered an American accent, began, 'Was that—?'

'Yes!' Tory confirmed and, half tripping over the Chinese take-away, picked the bags up and shoved them at Alex. 'Carry these in!'

Then she raced down the steps and across the street in time to catch Lucas Ryecart opening the door of the Range Rover.

'Wait, please,' she appealed before he could climb behind the steering wheel.

He stopped and turned. His expression was now remote, as if he'd already dismissed her from his mind, but, after a moment's deliberation, he closed the car door and leaned against it.

'Okay, I'm waiting.' He folded muscular sinewy arms across a broad chest.

Tory saw tension and anger beneath the apparently casual gesture. 'I...um...just wanted to clear up any possible misunderstanding. About Alex being there, I mean. You see…well, it's not—'

'How it seems?' he cut across her ramblings with a mocking lift of one dark brow.

'Yes, ' she confirmed, 'I mean, no, it isn't.'

'So that wasn't Alex Simpson,' he drawled on, 'and you aren't about to share an evening meal with him and he isn't currently staying at your flat and you haven't lied to me about your involvement with him.'

Tory saw from his face that she would be wasting her time, telling the truth. Any inclination on his part to kiss and make up had departed with Alex's appearance at the door.

'There's no point in this,' she muttered to herself and would have walked away if a hand hadn't shot out to keep her there.

She tried to pull her arm free. When she couldn't, she lifted her other hand, intending to push him away. He was too quick for her. He grabbed both her wrists and dragged her round until he had her backed against his car.

He did it with the minimum of force. Only her pride was really hurt.

She snapped at him, 'Let me go!'

'Okay.' He released her but stood so close she was still trapped and asked, 'Is Simpson's wife filing for divorce?'

She frowned at the unexpected question. 'Yes, possibly. Why?'

'Well, that explains the need to keep quiet,' he concluded, 'if not the attraction.'

His eyes narrowed in contempt and Tory found herself flaring back, 'You know nothing!'

'You're right. I don't,' he agreed in the same vein. 'I don't know why a bright, beautiful young woman would waste herself on a washed-up has-been with a wife, two kids and a drink habit to support… Perhaps you could enlighten me?'

'Alex isn't a has-been!' Tory protested angrily, recalling the programme outlines they'd prepared to impress this man. Some of their ideas were good, damn good. All futile, now, it would seem. 'And he doesn't have a drink problem.'

He threw her a look of pity.

'Who says love doesn't walk around with a white cane and guide dog?'

She threw him back a look of fury.

'I'm not in love with Alex Simpson! I never have been in love with Alex Simpson. I never shall be. I don't even believe in love!'

She spoke in no uncertain terms and speculation replaced pity in his gaze, but he still didn't release her.

'So you don't love Simpson,' he mused aloud. 'You don't love anybody. I wonder what gets you through the day, Tory Lloyd?'

'My work,' she answered, both literally and figuratively. 'That's what's important to me. That's *all* that's important to me.'

He shook his head, then leaned towards her to say in a low voice, 'If that's true, Simpson must be goddamn lousy in bed.'

Tory reacted with shocked disbelief. 'Do you have to be so...so...?'

'Accurate?'

'Crude!'

'I can't help it,' he claimed. 'I am American, after all.'

His tone was serious, but inside he was laughing. At her.

'Is that what you like about Simpson? Is he suitably re-fined?'

'More so than you, at any rate.'

Tory had, by this time, given up worrying about job security.

Lucas Ryecart had also abandoned any effort to be a fair, reasonable employer.

'I won't argue with that.' He shrugged off any insult, before drawling, 'But at least I have a certain homespun notion of morality.'

'Really?' Tory sniffed.

'Yes, really,' he echoed. 'If I were married, I wouldn't dump my wife and kids just because a newer, prettier model came along—'

'That's not the way it was,' Tory almost spat at him, 'and who knows what *you'd* do. You're *not* married, are you?'

'Not currently, but I was.' His face clouded briefly.

Tory could have kicked herself. She'd forgotten momentarily his connection with Jessica Wainwright.

'And when I was married, I was faithful,' he added quietly.

Tory believed him. He hadn't cheated on Jessica. He hadn't cheated because he'd adored her.

Her anger faded as she wondered if he still grieved but she didn't want to probe further. She was uncomfortable with the whole subject.

'Mr Ryecart,' she replied at length, 'I don't feel this is any of my business.'

'It will be, *Miss* Lloyd,' he mocked her formality, 'come the day I take you away from Simpson.'

'What?'

'I said—'

'I heard!' She just didn't believe him. Was it a joke?

Blue eyes caught and held hers. They told her it was no joke.

'I've decided I *am* interested, after all,' he stated dispassionately.

They could have been discussing a business deal. She was to be his latest acquisition. Take over, asset strip, move on.

'I thought you were too old for me,' Tory reminded him pointedly.

'I'd have said so, yes,' he agreed in dry tones, 'but as you're already living with someone of my advanced years, you obviously don't share my reservations.'

'I am *not* living with Alex,' she seethed in denial.

'You're simply good friends, right?' He slanted her a sceptical look.

Tory wanted to slap him. She longed to. She'd never had such a violent urge before.

'Oh, think what you like!' She finally snapped. 'Only don't take it out on Alex.'

'Meaning?' Dark brows lifted.

'Meaning: you may fancy me—' she continued angrily.

A deep, mocking laugh interrupted her. 'English understatement, I love it. I don't just *fancy* you, Miss Lloyd. I want you. I desire you. I'd like to—'

'Okay, I've got the picture,' she cut across him before he became any more explicit. 'But that's not my fault or Alex's. I haven't encouraged you. If this affects our positions at Eastwich—'

'You'll scream sexual harassment?' His eyes hardened.

Tory scowled in return. He was putting words in her mouth that weren't there. 'I wasn't saying that.'

'Good, because I've told you before,' he growled back, 'I am quite capable of separating my private life and my position as Chief Executive of Eastwich... If I decide to fire Simpson, you can be sure it'll be for a better reason than the fact he's currently sharing your bed.'

'He isn't!' Tory protested once more, only to draw a cynical glance that made her finally lose it. 'To hell with this! You're right, of course. Alex and I *are* lovers. In fact, we're at it like rabbits. Night and day. Every spare moment,' she ran on wildly. 'We can't keep our hands off each other.'

It silenced him, but only briefly before he drawled back, 'Now who's being crude?'

'It's called irony,' she countered.

'All right, so if you and Simpson aren't lovers...' he surmised aloud.

'Give the man a coconut,' she muttered under her breath.

He ignored her, finishing, 'Prove it!'

'*Prove it?*' she echoed in exasperation. 'And how am I meant to do that—set up a surveillance camera in my bedroom?'

'That would hardly cover it,' he responded coolly. 'Some couples rarely make it to the bedroom. I prefer outdoor sex myself. How about you?'

Tory didn't have to feign shock at an involuntary vision of a couple entwined in long grass under a blue sky. Not just any couple, either.

She shut her eyes to censor the image and heard his deep drawl continue, 'Not that I was suggesting it as an immediate option. A date will do, initially.'

Tory's eyes snapped open again. 'A date?'

'You know—' he smiled as if he could see inside her head '—boy asks girl out. Girl says yes. They go to a restaurant or the movies. Boy takes girl home. If he's lucky, he gets to kiss her. If he's very lucky, he gets to—'

'Yes, all right,' she snapped before he could warm any more to the theme. '*You're* asking *me* on a date?'

'That was the general idea,' he confirmed.

'To prove I'm not slee—having an affair with Alex?' Her tone told him how absurd she thought it.

'It isn't conclusive,' he admitted. 'But if you were my woman, I wouldn't let another man get too close. I reckon Alex Simpson will feel the same way.'

Tory doubted it. Even if she had been Alex's *woman*—how primitive it sounded—she didn't see Alex fighting anyone over her.

'Alex doesn't work like that,' she said disdainfully. 'He's much too civilised.'

'Really.' He glanced across the street towards her house and the bay window on the ground floor.

Tory followed his eyes in time to see Alex drawing back behind a net curtain. Evidently he'd been watching them. It was hardly surprising.

'He's curious, that's all,' she explained. 'He's realised who you are. It's nothing personal.'

'Yeah, I bet,' he scoffed in reply.

'It's true!' she insisted.

'Okay, so it's true,' he repeated, humouring her, 'in which case he won't mind if I do this.'

'Do wh—?' The question went unfinished.

The American leaned forward and kissed her before she could stop him. His lips touched hers with fleeting intimacy. It was over in a matter of seconds, but she was left feeling the imprint of his mouth on hers.

'I—I...' she stammered, wide-eyed '...you sh-shouldn't...'

'No, I shouldn't,' he agreed, gazing hard at her. 'But now I have...'

Now he had, he would have to kiss her again. His eyes told her that.

Tory had time to protest, turn her head, do anything but stand there looking up at him. Time to move away before his head blocked out the sun and his mouth covered hers, hard and possessive. Time to pull back as he began to kiss as if they were already lovers.

Only Tory had never felt like this before. Totally powerless, her eyes shutting, her lips parting, letting him in. Unable to resist as he stole the breath and the will from her. Boneless and fluid in strong arms wrapped round her waist, drawing her closer.

Passion flared so quickly, it caught them both unawares. Somewhere in the back of her head, Tory knew this was crazy, but she didn't seem to care. Her arms lifted to his shoulders and he dragged her body to his. They fell back against the side of his car, oblivious. He went on kissing her. He started touching her. They forgot where they were.

Her jacket was big for her. Just as well. It hid the movements of his hands, pulling out the T-shirt from her jeans, running up over her back, then round to her small, firm breasts. She wore a crop top rather than bra. He touched her above it, stroking a nipple erect through the material. She moaned in his mouth. He groaned back and tried to push aside the top. She didn't stop him. She wanted this.

Sanity returned only as the front door of the nearest house slammed and a voice exclaimed loudly, 'Look, Mummy, they're still kissing. Don't they know they'll get each other's germs?'

'Shh, Jack,' another instructed, 'and stop staring. Just get into the car!'

The first, childish voice penetrated the mush that Tory's brain had turned into, and the mother's had a sudden, sobering effect.

She pushed at Lucas Ryecart's shoulders. He'd already taken his hand from her breast but was slow to release her entirely. He lifted his head away and they both glanced in the direction of the woman hustling her child into a car parked some yards down the road.

Embarrassed colour filled Tory's cheeks but Lucas Ryecart was unflustered. He didn't hide his pleasure in the kiss but gave her a slow, sensuous smile.

'You'll come back with me.' It was a statement, not a question.

Tory looked blank.

'To my hotel.' He made his meaning clear.

And the blue eyes holding hers made it clearer still.

'I...of course not!' Tory finally mustered up some indignation.

He ignored it. 'Why not? We both want it.'

Tory shook her head, denying it.

He smiled, and the smile called her a liar. He thought her a pushover. Something to do with the fact she'd just acted like one.

Pride reasserted itself and she tried to pull free. He held her easily, large hands spanning her waist.

'You won't have to go back to Simpson,' he assured her. 'I'll help you move out on him tomorrow.'

Tory stared back at him. What was he suggesting?

'We've only just met.' Her tone told him he was absurd.

'So?' He laughed. 'How often does it feel like this?'

She could have said, *Like what?* but he might have reminded her. And she didn't need it. Her body was trembling from the simple touch of his hand on her waist.

'You don't have to move in with me,' he went on. 'Not yet, at any rate. But you can't keep living with Simpson.'

'I'm not living with Alex,' she repeated for what seemed like the twentieth time. 'It's my flat.'

'Even easier,' he reasoned. '*You* can kick *him* out.'

Tory discounted the kiss and finally asked herself why she was having this conversation with a perfect stranger.

'You're crazy,' she concluded with more than a vein of seriousness.

'No, *I'm* honest,' he countered, 'and I don't see much point in fighting the inevitable.'

Him and her in bed together. That was what he meant. Tory didn't need a translation. His eyes told her. His certainty was disturbing. He imagined she was so easy.

It was time to fight back.

'Mr Ryecart—' she gave him a look that would have soured cream '—you either think an awful lot of yourself or very little of me. Whichever, I would sooner walk over red-hot coals with a plastic petrol can in my hand than go to bed with you. Is that honest enough for you?'

Was it insulting enough? Tory asked herself.

Seemingly not as he made some sound of disbelief and she, losing her temper, pushed him hard on the chest.

Taken by surprise, he stumbled backwards but recovered in time to grab her as she tried to escape.

The smile was gone. His eyes glittered dangerously. 'You can't sleep with Simpson again. Do you understand?'

A shiver went down Tory's back at the unspoken threat. She pulled at her arm but he wouldn't release her.

'Do you understand?' he repeated.

'Yes,' she choked the word out.

He caught and held her eyes, insisting, 'You *won't* sleep with him,' even as he finally let her go.

For a moment Tory returned his stare, and saw something in it, dark and disturbing, that told her she didn't really know who this man was.

Then she was running, running as she should have done earlier, blindly across the road and up the steps, through the door Alex had left on the latch.

She didn't look back. If she had, she would have seen him.

Lucas Ryecart watched her until the moment she disappeared.

CHAPTER FOUR

TORY'S office looked out onto the main corridor. Monday morning she watched Alex and the other senior producers walk towards the conference room at the far end. They were in subdued mood for their first official meeting with the new big chief.

Two hours later she watched them return with a considerably more relaxed air.

Only Alex didn't. He didn't return for another half an hour.

Simon spotted him first. 'Here he is.'

Alex popped his head round the door. 'Tory, can I see you for a moment?'

His manner gave little away as he proceeded to his office.

'Maybe he wants help in clearing his desk,' suggested Simon on a hopeful note.

Tory muttered, 'Shut up, Simon,' in passing as she walked past him on her way to Alex's office, closing the door behind her.

'Everything all right?' she asked tentatively, then listened in bemusement as Alex began to enthuse over the American and his plans for Eastwich.

It was as if he had suffered a blinding conversion on the road to Damascus with Lucas Ryecart in the role of God.

'When he asked me to wait back,' Alex ran on, 'I thought, This is it. The axe is about to fall. But nothing. He just wanted to discuss the direction I envisaged our department taking.'

Tory's gaze was incredulous. Did Alex really believe Ryecart was interested in his opinions?

'Naturally I handed over the presentation package I'd prepared,' he declared smugly. 'He seemed impressed.'

'Really.' Tory tried to convey some of her scepticism.

Alex misunderstood. 'Don't worry, he knows you had a part

in it. He asked me how long we'd worked in such close liaison.'

Tory recognised sarcasm even if Alex didn't and could have groaned aloud. She wondered how she could bring Alex up to speed. The trouble was she'd worked hard to kill Alex's curiosity about Ryecart the evening before. She'd put their evident quarrel down to the American's belief that she'd been less than honest about Alex's whereabouts and fortunately Alex hadn't witnessed the kiss that had followed.

'I wouldn't take what he says at face value, Alex,' she warned at length.

But Alex refused to let her dampen his spirits. 'He seems straight enough to me... Anyway, I feel like celebrating. Come to lunch. Antoine's. My treat.'

Tory wondered how Alex could suddenly afford to pay for such extravagant dining.

'Thanks,' Tory replied, 'but I have an appointment in less than an hour. We could go to the canteen, if you like.'

Alex pulled a face, as Tory had guessed he would, and said, 'I'll pass, if you don't mind.'

'Not at all.' Tory trailed back to her office, still puzzling over Ryecart's game plan.

'Well?' Simon enquired as she returned.

'Everything's fine,' Tory said succinctly and went to pick up her bag from under her chair. 'I'm going to the canteen for lunch.'

'I'll come with you.' Simon wanted to hear more.

They walked along the corridor together and she relayed some of the phrases Alex had used about the American while Simon raised a sceptical brow.

'Miss Lloyd!' Someone called from behind them.

Tory kept walking for a step or two, pretending she hadn't heard. She had no need to glance round to identify the voice.

'Wait up.' Simon grabbed her arm. 'It's the man himself.'

'You don't say!' Her teeth were already clenched as she turned to find Lucas Ryecart bearing down on them.

It was a purely physical reaction. She knew she didn't like him. She'd told herself that a hundred times.

But it had changed nothing. Her heart still stopped for a beat or two, then raced like a runaway train. She heard its engine roar and tried to focus on her dislike, not his looks. Did all women feel the same? Was that why he'd been called God's gift?

Their absorption in each other was mutual and obvious, so much so that Simon said, 'Shall I make myself scarce?'

'Yes!'

'No!'

The answers were simultaneous, but Simon knew which side his bread was buttered. He smiled at Eastwich's new boss before strolling off down the corridor.

Deserted, Tory went on the offensive. 'What do you want?'

'We need to talk,' he responded in a low undertone, 'but not here. It's too public. Come to lunch.'

Tory shook her head. 'I can't.'

'Or won't?' he challenged in reply.

Tory had forgotten he had no time for social niceties. She abandoned them, too.

'All right, I won't,' she confirmed.

He nodded, then looked at her long and hard. 'If it's any comfort, you scare the hell out of me, too.'

Was he serious? Tory wasn't sure, but the conversation was already in dangerous territory.

She deliberately misunderstood him, answering, 'I don't know why you'd be scared of me, Mr Ryecart. It's not as if *I* could sack *you*.'

He made an exasperated sound. 'That's not what I meant and you know it! Can't you forget our respective positions for a single moment?'

'Shh!' she urged before they attracted an audience. 'But, no, since you ask, I can't forget. Neither would you, I imagine, if you were in my position.'

'Underneath me?' he suggested.

'Yes!' She'd walked right into it.

He smiled, giving it a whole new meaning, while Tory blushed furiously.

'If only you were.' His eyes made a leisurely trip down her body and back again.

'You—' Tory could think of several names to call him but none seemed rude enough.

'It's all right, I can guess.' He was more amused than anything.

Tory seethed with frustration and anger. If she didn't walk away, she would surely hit him.

She did walk away, but he followed her to the lift.

It took an age to arrive. She stood there, ignoring him. Which was hard, when she could feel him staring at her.

The lift arrived and a couple of women from Drama stepped out. They nodded at Tory, then glanced at her companion. Their gaze was one of admiration rather than recognition.

Lucas Ryecart was oblivious, stepping into the lift with her.

Tory wanted to step out again, but it seemed an act of cowardice. What could he do in the five seconds it took for the lift to reach the ground floor?

He could stop it, that was what. He could run a quick eye over the array of buttons and hit the emergency one.

Tory didn't quite realise what he'd done until the lift lurched to a halt.

'You can't do that!' She was genuinely outraged at his action.

'Why not?'

'I…you… Because…well, you just can't!'

He grinned, mocking her regard for authority, and she flashed him a look of dislike.

'Don't worry,' he assured her, 'I'll give myself a severe reprimand later… For now, let's talk.'

'I don't want to talk.' Tory eyed the control panel, wondering if she should make a lunge at it.

She rejected the move as overly dramatic until he drawled, 'Fair enough. Let's not talk,' and, with one step, closed the distance between them.

Sensual blue eyes warned her of his intention.

Tory's heart leapt. In alarm, she decided, and raised her arms to fend him off.

'If you touch me—'

'You'll scream?'

So she wasn't original. She was still serious.

'Yes!'

'Well, of course, what else would you do, the lift being stuck and all?'

Tory glowered at him. He had an answer for everything.

He stretched out a hand and lightly brushed a strand of hair from her cheek. Then, before she could protest, he stepped back to his corner of the lift.

'Don't panic. I won't touch you till you ask me to.'

He appeared confident she would.

'We'll both be dead before then,' she shot back.

The insult went wide. His smile remained.

He leaned back against the wall as if he had all the time in the world. 'You never told Simpson about our...our *conversation* yesterday, did you?'

'There was nothing to tell,' she retorted, the ultimate put-down.

He arched a brow in disbelief. 'It's fairly usual for you, I suppose, being propositioned by other men?'

'Happens all the time,' she claimed, deadpan.

He laughed, briefly amused, then regarded her intently before murmuring, 'I can believe it.'

He had a way of looking at a woman that made Tory finally understand the expression 'bedroom eyes'. She tried hard to conjure up some indignation.

He helped her along by adding, 'So why settle for a wimp like Simpson?'

'When I could have someone like you?' she replied with obvious scorn.

'I wasn't thinking specifics. Pretty much any young, free and single guy would be an improvement on Simpson,' he said in considered tones. 'But, yes, since you're asking, I reckon there's every chance you could have me.'

The sheer nerve of him took Tory's breath away. 'You...I...wasn't—'

'After you show Simpson the door, of course,' he stated as a condition.

Tory still didn't believe she was having this conversation. 'And if I don't?'

His eyes narrowed, even as he admitted, 'I haven't thought that far.'

But when he did? Would their jobs be in jeopardy?

Tory found it impossible to gauge. Lucas Ryecart was still a stranger to her.

She glanced across at him. Today he was dressed formally. In dark double-breasted suit, relieved by a white shirt and silk tie, he would have looked every inch the businessman if it hadn't been for his casual stance, hands in pockets, length resting against a wall of the lift.

He caught and held her eye and homed in on her thoughts as he continued, 'If I wanted to fire Alex Simpson, I could have done so this morning with no great effort. I believe he has already had the requisite number of warnings.'

Tory hadn't known that. She'd imagined the executive board of Eastwich ignorant of Alex's recent conduct.

'Had you and he *not* been cohabiting—' his mouth twisted on the word '—chances are I would have. Instead I felt obliged to keep carrying him, at least for the time being.'

Tory frowned, failing to follow his logic. 'I don't understand.'

'It's like this. I *wanted* to fire him and normally would have.' A shrug said it would have given him little grief. 'However, I wasn't a hundred per cent certain why. Most likely it was because he's a sorry excuse for a production manager, but it just could be because he happens to be living with the woman I want,' he pondered aloud.

'I—I…y-you…' His bluntness reduced Tory to incoherence.

'So I decided I'd leave it for now,' he concluded, 'and if he continues to mess up, I won't have the dilemma.'

'You'll fire him, anyway?' Tory finally found her voice.

'Correct,' he confirmed without apology.

'And what if he gets back on form?' she challenged.

'Then he has nothing to worry about it.' He met her eye and his gaze did not waver.

He was either a man of honour or a very convincing liar. The jury was still out on which, but Tory could see the situation was going to be impossible.

'Maybe I should be the one to leave.'

'Eastwich?'

'Yes.'

His face darkened momentarily. 'You'd do that for Simpson?'

The suggestion had Tory sighing loudly. 'You mean hand in my notice while quoting "It is a far, far better thing that I do," etc. etc.?'

His lips quirked slightly, recognising the irony in her voice. 'Something like that.'

'Well, I'm sorry to disappoint you, but self-sacrifice is not part of my nature,' she told him. 'Try self-preservation.'

'From me?' He arched a brow.

'Who else?' she flipped back.

Arms folded, he thought about it some, before querying, 'Do I bother you that much?'

'Yes. No... What do you expect?' she retorted in quick succession and masked any confusion with a glare.

It had little effect. 'I must say, you bother me, too, Miss Lloyd. Here I am, supposed to be rescuing Eastwich from economic collapse, and I can't get my mind off one of its production assistants... What's a man meant to do?' he appealed with a smile that was slow and lazy and probably intended to devastate.

But Tory was wise to him now. 'This is all a joke to you, isn't it?'

'A joke?' he reflected. 'I wouldn't say so. Well, no more than life is generally.'

So that was his philosophy: life was a joke. It was hardly reassuring. For her or Eastwich.

'It comes with age,' he added at her silence.

'What does?'

'The realisation that nothing should be taken too seriously, least of all life.'

'Thank you,' Tory replied dryly, 'but I'd prefer to make up my own mind—when I grow up, of course.'

'Was I being patronising?'

'Just a shade.'

'Sorry.'

He pulled an apologetic face and Tory found herself smiling in response.

'Rare but definitely beautiful,' he murmured at this momentary lapse.

Tory tried hard not to feel flattered and counteracted with a scowl.

'Too late.' He read her mind all too well.

'Could you restart the lift…please?' she said in a tight voice. 'I'd like to go to lunch.'

'Sure,' he agreed to her surprise and reset the emergency stop.

The lift geared into action rather suddenly and Tory lurched forward at the same time. She was in no danger of falling but Lucas Ryecart caught her all the same.

He held her while she regained her balance. Then he went on holding her, even as the lift descended smoothly.

She wore a sleeveless shift dress. His hands were warm on her skin. She still shivered at the lightness of his touch.

She could have protested. She tried. She raised her head but the words didn't come. It was the way he was looking at her—or looking at his own hands, smoothing over her soft skin, imagining.

When he finally lifted his eyes to hers, he didn't hide his feelings. He desired her. Now.

He drew her to him, and she went, as if she had no volition. Only she did: she wanted him to kiss her, willed him to. Needed it. Turned into his arms. Gazed up at him, eyes wary, but expectant.

The lift came to a halt even as he cupped her face in his hands and lowered his mouth to hers. By the time the door slid open, he was kissing her thoroughly and she was help-lessly responding.

'Well!' The exclamation came from one of the two men standing on the other side.

Too late Tory sprang apart from Lucas to face Colin Mathieson and a tall, grey-haired man of indeterminate age.

Colin's surprise became shock when Lucas turned to face them also.

The stranger, however, appeared greatly amused.

'We've been looking for you, Lucas, boy,' he drawled, 'but obviously not in the right places.'

He chuckled and his eyes slid to Tory, openly admiring Lucas's taste.

'Chuck,' Lucas responded, quite unfazed, 'this is—'

But Tory, horrified and humiliated, wasn't going to hang around while he introduced her to his American buddy.

'Don't bother!' she snapped at him, and took off.

She heard Colin call after her, half reprimand, half concern. She heard the stranger laugh loudly, as if enjoying the situation. She heard nothing from Lucas Ryecart but she could well imagine that slow, slanting smile of satisfaction.

Yet again, he had proved his point. Good sense might tell her he was like a disease—seriously bad for her health—but she seemed to have little immunity. The only sane thing was to keep out of infection range.

She went to the staff canteen, certain he wouldn't follow her there.

'Where have you been?' Simon demanded when she sat down with a spartan meal of salad and orange juice. 'I was about to give you up for dead—or alternatively *bed*. I wonder if he looks at all women that way.'

'Shut up, Simon,' she muttered repressively.

But Simon was unstoppable. 'Talk about smouldering. I used to think that was just an expression. Like in women's novels: "He gave her a dark, smouldering look." But not since I saw Ryecart—'

'*Simon!*' Tory glanced round and was relieved to see no one within listening distance. 'You might think this sort of thing is funny but I doubt Lucas Ryecart would. You have heard of libel, I assume.'

'Slander,' Simon corrected. 'I haven't written it down… Well, not yet.'

'What do you mean, not yet?' Tory told herself he was joking.

Simon grinned. 'I could scribble it on the washroom wall, I suppose. L loves T. Or is it T loves L?' he said with a speculative air.

'It's neither,' she replied, teeth gritted.

Simon arched a surprised brow at her tone, but he took the hint and changed the subject.

Tory didn't linger over the meal but returned on her own to the office and threw herself into work so she wouldn't have to think too hard about anything else.

Alex didn't return from lunch—it seemed he was bent on pushing his luck—but she told herself firmly it wasn't her problem. She worked late as usual and was emerging from the front door just as Colin Mathieson was stowing his briefcase in the back of his car.

As he was a senior executive his bay was right at the entrance and, short of going back inside, she couldn't avoid him.

'Tory.' He greeted her with a friendly enough smile. 'I'm glad I've run into you. I wanted a word.'

Tory waited. She didn't prompt him. She just hoped the word wasn't about what she suspected.

She hoped in vain and stood there, wanting the ground to swallow her up, as Colin Mathieson gave her an avuncular talk which, while skirting round the point, could basically be summed up as: You are lowly, young production assistant. He is rich, charming man of the world. Are you sure you know what you're doing?

It was well meant, which was why Tory managed to mutter 'yes' and 'no' in the right places and somehow contain her feelings until she could scream aloud in the privacy of her own car.

Because it was galling. To be thought such a fool. Colin actually believed she was so naive that she took Lucas Ryecart seriously.

The day she did that, she really was in trouble.

CHAPTER FIVE

AFTER the lift incident, Tory was determined to avoid Lucas Ryecart. It proved easy. The American spent the next day closeted in meetings with various departments before disappearing to the States for the rest of the week.

His absence put things into perspective for Tory. While she'd been fretting over their next meeting, he'd been on a plane somewhere, with his mind on deals and dollars. Perhaps he did want her, but in the same way he'd want any grown-up toy, like a fast car or a yacht. He'd spare a little time for it, enjoy it a while, then move onto something—or someone—new.

She'd almost managed to get him out of her head when the postcard arrived with a bundle of other mail on the Saturday morning.

There was no name on it, just a picture of the Statue of Liberty on one side and the words, 'Has he gone?' on the other.

'Are you all right?' Alex noticed her strained expression across the breakfast table.

'Yes, fine.' She quickly shoved it in among her other letters. 'It...it's just a card from my mother.'

'I thought she'd moved to Australia,' Alex commented.

Realising he'd seen the picture side, she was committed to another lie. 'She's on holiday in New York.'

Alex nodded and quickly lost interest.

Tory reflected on the words in the postcard. *Has he gone?* How she wished!

She slid a glance at Alex, currently unsetting all the stations on her radio. He was driving her crazy.

Fanatically *un*tidy, he left clothes on chairs, take-away cartons on tables and used towels on floors.

61

Tory had tried a few subtle hints, then more direct comments and he was suitably contrite—but not enough to reform.

Tory wondered if it were her. Maybe she wasn't suited to cohabitation, even on platonic grounds.

At any rate, she longed for Alex to depart. Or had until the postcard had arrived. Now she was torn. She didn't want to seem to be giving into Lucas Ryecart's demands.

In the end she let fate decide it and when Alex returned later that day from an unsuccessful flat-finding mission she surprised him with her concession to stay a little longer.

'You're a star. I'll try to look for a place mid-week,' Alex promised, 'although it might be difficult, with Ryecart returning on Monday.'

Tory pulled a face. 'He's definitely back?'

'Didn't I say?' Alex ran on. 'He sent a fax yesterday, setting up a meeting with our department. Monday morning at the Abbey Lodge.'

'No, you didn't say.' Tory struggled to hide her irritation.

'Don't worry about it,' he dismissed. 'He just wants to discuss the department's future direction.'

'Well, I'll keep a low profile,' she rejoined, 'if it's all the same to you.'

Alex didn't argue. Having been bullied into sobriety by Tory, he had regained some of his old ambition. He would be too busy promoting his own career to spare much thought for Tory's.

In fact, come Monday morning, it was a two-man contest between Simon and Alex.

Simon gained an early lead by simply turning up on time. Caught by roadworks, Alex and Tory were already fifteen minutes late when they reached the Abbey Lodge Hotel and entered the lion's den.

Tory refused to look at the lion even when he drawled a polite, 'Good morning,' in her direction.

It was a small conference room, mostly taken up with an oval table and eight leather chairs. She put Simon between her and the great man, and left Alex to sit opposite and run through a quick explanation for their tardiness.

It did have some semblance to the truth. Alex's car *was* in the garage. She *had* given him a lift. And they hadn't anticipated the council digging up a major section of the ring road.

But, of course, Lucas Ryecart knew the reality: that Alex and she had arrived together because they were living together.

He even gave Alex the chance to confess. 'Do you and Tory live in the same neighbourhood?'

'I...no, not really.' Alex slid a conspiratorial glance in Tory's direction.

He was doing as he'd promised by keeping quiet about their current arrangement.

Tory's heart sank as Lucas drawled, 'That was *generous* of you, Tory, to go out of your way,' and forced her to look at him.

It had been a week since they'd met and in the interim she'd put herself through aversion therapy. She *could* not like this man, brash egotist that he was. She *would* not like this man, even if her job depended on it. She *had* to look at him with dispassion and see the ruthlessness that underlay the handsome features.

This time she was ready—just not ready enough. She saw his age, written in his sun-lined face and the grey round his temples. She saw the imperfection, a scar tracing white down one cheek. She saw the mouth set in an irritatingly mocking curve. But then she met his eyes and forgot the rest.

A deep blue, bluer than a tropical sky, they drew her to him, those eyes, and made her realise that attraction defied any logic. The sight of him still left her senses in turmoil.

But this time she fought it, this involuntary attraction. She got angry with herself for such weakness. She got even angrier with him for causing it.

'Actually, it wasn't out of my way at all.' Her voice held a defiant note.

His mouth straightened to a hard line. He understood immediately. She was answering his postcard. No, Alex hasn't gone.

He went on staring at her until she was forced to look away, then he switched back to business.

He talked frankly of the direction he envisaged the department taking. He wished to concentrate on documentaries with a longer shelf-life. Previous programmes had suffered from delays and hence loss of topicality or duplication from other companies.

Alex clearly felt he was being told what he already knew. 'We are conscious of duplication,' he put in. 'We abandoned a project not so long ago because Tyne Tees was further along on it.'

'How much did that cost Eastwich?' Lucas Ryecart enquired.

'I can't remember,' Alex admitted.

'I can.' Lucas Ryecart stated a figure.

'Sounds right,' Alex said rather too casually. 'Budgets aren't normally my concern.'

Tory, assiduously contemplating the wood grain in front of her, flinched inwardly. Did Alex have to jump into the hole the American was digging for him?

There was a moment's silence before Ryecart returned briefly, 'So I gathered.'

Alex caught on then, and backtracked to make the right sounds, 'Not that I don't try to work within a budget framework. In fact, some programmes have been done on a shoestring.'

'Really.' Lucas Ryecart's disbelief was dry but obvious. 'Okay, surprise me!'

'Sorry?' Alex blinked.

'Which programme was done on a shoestring?'

'I…well…' Alex was left to bluster. 'That's an expression. Obviously I didn't mean it literally, but I believe we're no more profligate than any other department. Look at drama.' He tried to shift focus. 'It's common knowledge that their last period piece cost half a million.'

'And made double that by the time Eastwich had sold it abroad.' Lucas Ryecart pointed out what Alex would have known if he'd thought about it. 'Moving on, Alex has drafted some proposals for future programmes with which I assume you're all familiar.'

Tory assumed the same but, from his tight-lipped expression, Simon was still in the dark.

'I left a copy on top of your desk,' Alex claimed at his blank expression.

'Really.' Simon was clearly unimpressed with Alex's efforts, and Tory didn't blame him.

'Have mine.' She pushed the document towards him. 'I have a spare.'

'Simon, you can get up to speed while we discuss it,' Lucas Ryecart pressed on. 'Okay, folks, at the risk of riding roughshod over anyone's pet project, I propose we can items one and four from the outset.'

'Can?' Alex echoed in supercilious tones although Tory was sure he understood.

'Rule out, bin, expunge.' Lucas Ryecart gave him a selection of alternatives that somehow made Alex look the fool.

Certainly Simon allowed himself a smirk.

Alex came back with, 'Why…if I may ask?'

His tone implied the American was being dictatorial.

'You can ask, yes.' Lucas Ryecart clearly considered Alex pompous rather than challenging. 'Proposal one is too close to a programme about to be broadcast by BBC2 and the costs on four will be sky high.'

Tory watched Alex's face as he woke up to the fact that the American was going to be no pushover like Colin Mathieson.

'Costs are the only criterion?' he said in the tone of the artist thwarted by commercialism.

Lucas Ryecart was unmoved. 'With Eastwich's current losses, yes. But if you want to spend your own money on it, Alex, feel free.'

He said it with a smile but the message was plain enough. Put up or shut up.

Alex looked thunderous while Simon gloated.

'Proposal two…' Lucas Ryecart barely paused '…is also likely to attract mega-buck litigation unless we can substantiate every claim we make against the drug companies.'

'You know that's damn near impossible,' Alex countered. 'We'd have to rely on inside sources, any of whom could be less than truthful.'

'Exactly,' Lucas Ryecart agreed, 'so I'd sooner pass... However, should you wish to take the story elsewhere, I won't stand in your way.'

Alex went from indignant to disconcerted as the American threw him off balance again. He had yet to fully appreciate that behind the pleasant drawling voice there was a man of steel.

'So that leaves us two ideas still on the table,' he resumed. 'Racial discrimination in the Armed Forces and drug-taking in the playground. Either might be worth exploring... In addition, Simon and I both have an idea we'd like to pitch.'

Alex was instantly suspicious. 'The same one?'

'Actually, no.' It was Simon who answered. 'We don't all go in for the conspiratorial approach.'

His disparaging glance included Tory. He'd obviously lined her up on Alex's side. She might have protested, had Lucas Ryecart not been there and likely to scorn any claim of impartiality.

'Tory—' the American turned those brilliant blue eyes on her '—perhaps you have some idea you'd like to put forward as well.'

She already had: at least two of Alex's proposals had originated with her, but, in giving them to Alex, she had effectively lost copyright.

She shook her head, and wondered if he considered her gormless. She had certainly contributed little to the meeting so far.

'As you know, Tory and I worked quite closely on this document.' Alex imagined he was rescuing her from obscurity.

Instead he confirmed what Simon suspected: that they'd worked as a team, excluding him.

It also made Ryecart drawl, 'Very closely, I understand.'

'I...well...yes...' Alex couldn't quite gauge the other man's attitude.

Tory could, only too well. For *very closely* read *intimately*.

She was finally stirred into retaliation. 'Have you a problem with that, Mr Ryecart?'

He fronted her in return. 'Not at all. I look forward to working in close liaison with you myself, Miss Lloyd.'

And let that be a lesson to me, Tory thought, clenching her teeth at the barely hidden double meaning.

She looked to the other two men, but if she expected any support she was in for a disappointment. Alex had put the American's comment down to sexist humour and was chuckling at it, and Simon was enjoying her discomfort.

It was every man for himself.

'Returning to the matter in hand,' Lucas Ryecart continued, 'I suggest each of us pitch our idea for a limited period, say forty minutes.'

He took his watch off and laid it on the table. It was a plain leather-strapped, gold-rimmed affair, nothing ostentatious. If Lucas Ryecart was wealthy, he didn't advertise the fact.

He glanced round the table, waiting for someone to volunteer. No one did. In adversity, they were suddenly a team.

'We're not used to working with time restraints,' Alex objected for all of them.

'I appreciate that, but I find deadlines cut down on bull,' Ryecart said bluntly, 'and forty minutes is the air-time for most documentaries produced at Eastwich... I'll go first, unless anyone objects.'

No one did. Tory felt a little ashamed for them all. They were such rabbits.

'Okay,' he proceeded. 'My idea more or less dropped in my lap. One of our backers, Chuck Wiseman, is a major publisher in the US and is looking to spread his empire to the UK. Specifically, he's bought out two quality women's magazines—*Toi* and *Vitalis*. Anyone read them?'

Tory was the only one to say, 'Yes.'

'Your opinion?' he asked seriously.

She answered in the same vein. '*Toi* is a pale imitation of *Marie Claire*. *Vitalis* is mainly hair, nails and make-up, with the occasional social conscience article.'

'Cynical but accurate.' He nodded in agreement. 'Chuck intends amalgamating the two, keeping the best of both and hoping to create something more original. But it is something of a marriage of convenience, with neither in any hurry to get to the altar.'

'It'll never work,' Alex commented.

'Possibly not,' Ryecart echoed, 'but Chuck's determined and he's a man to be reckoned with.'

'So where do we come in?' Tory was intrigued despite herself. 'Fly-on-the-wall stuff, recording the honeymoon.'

'Sort of,' Ryecart confirmed. 'Chuck's sending both staff on a residential weekend in the hope that familiarity will breed contentment.'

'He's obviously not very hot on old sayings,' Alex commented dryly.

'Still, it might make for a good story.' Simon smiled as he considered the in-fighting that would ensue. 'Where's he sending them? If it's somewhere hot and sunny, you can put me down for that one.'

Ryecart smiled briefly. ''Fraid not, Simon, but I'll note your enthusiasm. It's an outdoor-activity course in the Derbyshire Dales.'

'He has to be kidding!' Tory exclaimed before she could stop herself.

'Yeah, that's what I thought,' Ryecart echoed, 'but Chuck reckons he'll end up with a solid team as a result.'

'If they don't kill each other first,' murmured Simon.

'Or kill themselves, falling off a mountain,' Tory added. 'These courses are fairly rigorous, physically and psychologically.'

'Which is where we come in,' Ryecart rejoined.

'An exposé?' Tory enquired.

He nodded. 'Assuming there's anything to expose. Who knows? The course might be as character and team building as it claims.'

'I would think it would be more divisive,' Tory judged, but saw what he saw, too—the makings of a good human-interest story. 'I mean, if the staff know it's a test, there's going to be tension from the outset.'

He nodded. 'Two groups of individuals spending a weekend in each other's company under difficult circumstances. As fly-on-the-wall TV, it could prove dynamite.'

Alex and Simon nodded too, warming to the idea, even though it wasn't theirs.

'What are we talking here?' Alex asked. 'One of us plus camera crew interviewing these women while they abseil down mountains?'

'No crew,' Ryecart dismissed. 'The centre has continuous camera surveillance and uses camcorders for outdoor events. This footage will be handed over to Chuck's organisation and then to us.'

'Is that legal?' Simon said doubtfully.

'The centre has already signed a waiver, handing over copyright to Chuck,' Ryecart explained. 'The plan is for an Eastwich reporter to go undercover as a new member of staff for *Toi*. They'll have to join the magazine pretty much straight away as the course is this weekend. Whoever goes—' he glanced between the three of them '—I'll drive him or her down to London today for the interview.'

Both Simon and Alex looked at Tory.

'Why me?' She dreaded the idea of a car journey spent with Lucas Ryecart.

'At the risk of stating the obvious,' Simon drawled, 'they're both *women's* magazines. You're a woman. Alex and I aren't.'

'Quite.' Alex supported Simon for once.

Heart sinking, Tory looked towards the American.

He just said, 'It can be decided later,' and switched subjects with, 'Right, who wants to pitch their idea now?'

'I will.' Alex got in before Simon and began to flesh out his idea revolving drugs in the playground.

Alex had a somewhat novel idea, centring his investigation around public schools and the suggestion that a new breed of parents, themselves party-going and pill-popping in their youth, were tacitly condoning their children's drug-taking.

He'd obviously done some research on the subject and claimed to have already made contact with a headmaster willing to co-operate.

Simon cast doubt on the likelihood of that, pointing out that no public school head was likely to help him if it put fees at jeopardy.

'And you would know this, having gone to somewhere like Eton yourself?' Alex threw back.

'I did go to a public school, yes,' Simon said in his usual superior manner.

'A minor, I bet,' Alex guessed, accurately.

'Whereas you, no doubt, were a state grammar school boy,' Simon sneered back.

Tory suspected Simon already knew that, too. Alex was very proud of the fact.

'So?' Alex eyed Simon in an openly hostile manner.

'It shows, that's all,' Simon smirked in reply.

Exasperated, Tory intervened with a dry, 'Well, if anyone's interested, I went to a London comprehensive. Unofficial motto: Do it to them before they do it to you... But I was hoping I'd left my schooldays behind.'

Both Alex and Simon looked taken aback, as if a pet lapdog had suddenly produced fangs.

But it drew a slanting smile from Lucas Ryecart as he realised she was ridiculing their one-upmanship.

She didn't smile back. Simon and Alex might be behaving like prats but the American was still the common enemy.

'Quite,' Alex agreed at length and resumed speaking on his pet project while Simon continued to snipe the occasional remark and Lucas Ryecart refereed.

Tory wondered what the American made of the antipathy between the two men. Perhaps he was harbouring some idea of sending *their* fragmented team on an outdoor-activity course. The idea of Alex and Simon orienteering their way round some desolate Scottish moor, with only one compass between them, made her smile for the first time that day.

'You don't share that view?' a voice broke into her thoughts.

Tory looked up to find Lucas Ryecart's eyes on her again. Having only the vaguest idea of what had gone before, she hedged, 'I wouldn't say that exactly.'

'No, but your smile was a shade sceptical.' It seemed he'd been watching her.

'Possibly,' she admitted, rather than confess she'd been day-dreaming.

'So you don't agree with Alex that most adults under forty will have tried some kind of recreational drug?' he pursued.

Now she knew what they'd been discussing, Tory wasn't any more inclined to express an opinion.

'Tory won't have,' Simon chimed in. 'Far too strait-laced, aren't you, Tory? Doesn't smoke. Doesn't drink. Doesn't pretty much anything.'

'Shut up, Simon,' she responded without much hope he would.

'See... She doesn't even swear.' He grinned like a mischievous schoolboy. 'I somehow doubt her parents were pot-smoking flower children.'

'Well, that's where you're wrong!' Tory snapped without considering the wisdom of it.

She regretted her outburst almost immediately as all eyes in the room became trained on her.

'Would you care to expand on that?' invited Simon.

'No,' she ground back, 'I wouldn't.'

'But if it gives some insight into the subject—' he baited, amused rather than malignant.

'Simon.' A low warning, it came from Lucas Ryecart. 'Leave it.'

Tory should have been grateful. He'd seen her vulnerability. But didn't that make her even more vulnerable—to him rather than Simon?

'Sure.' Simon was wise enough not to want to make an enemy of the American. 'I didn't mean to tread on anyone's toes.'

'That makes a change,' Alex muttered in not so low a voice, then gave Tory a supportive smile.

Ryecart took control once more, 'Simon, would you like to pitch your idea now?'

'My pleasure.' Simon was obviously confident.

Tory listened to him outlining his idea for a docu-soap on

a day in the life of a Member of Parliament. It sounded pretty tame stuff until Simon named the backbencher he proposed using. A controversial figure, with intolerant views, he was likely to produce some interesting television.

'He's almost bound to be de-selected next time around,' Simon concluded, 'so he has nothing to lose.'

'Has he agreed to it?' Ryecart asked.

'Pretty much,' Simon confirmed.

'Know him personally?' Alex suggested.

'As a matter of fact, yes,' Simon responded. 'I was at school with his younger brother.'

Alex contented himself with a snort in comment.

Simon expanded on the approach he'd take and Lucas Ryecart gave him approval to progress it further. He had done the same for Alex.

He wrapped up the meeting by saying, 'All right, we'll meet again in three weeks and see where matters stand. Thank you for coming.'

They were dismissed. At least Tory thought they were, and was breathing a sigh of relief as she picked up her briefcase and led the way from the room. They were out in the hotel lobby when the American said, 'Tory, I'd like to talk to you.'

He didn't stipulate why but he didn't need to. He was her boss.

Alex looked ready to ask but Lucas Ryecart ran on, 'Simon, perhaps you could give Alex a ride back to Eastwich as his car is in the shop?'

'Sure, no problem.' Simon knew better than to object.

Alex, too, accepted the arrangement and Tory was abandoned altogether. That was how it felt, at any rate, as they walked out of the main entrance.

She guessed Lucas either wanted to talk to her about the magazine assignment or her current living arrangements, *vis-à-vis* Alex. Neither prospect was appealing.

'We can talk over lunch.' He began steering her by the elbow.

'In the dining room?' Tory wasn't dressed for five-star lunching.

'We could have a bar meal,' he continued, 'or call room service if you prefer.'

'Room service?' Tory echoed rather stupidly.

'I'm staying here,' he reminded her.

She stopped in her tracks. 'You expect me to go upstairs with you?'

'Expect, no,' he replied, 'hope, absolutely.'

His smile was more amused than lascivious. He just loved yanking her chain.

'So what's it to be?' he added.

'I'm not hungry!' she countered.

'Bar meal it is, then,' he decided for them and switched direction.

'I said—' She was about to repeat it.

He cut across her. 'I heard. You may not be hungry but I am, so you can sit and watch me eat while we talk business.'

Business. The word reminded her once more of their prospective positions. She wondered why she kept forgetting.

'Couldn't we just return to the conference room?' She wanted to keep things on a formal basis.

'And risk being alone together?' He raised a brow. 'Well, if that's okay with you—'

'No.' She hastily changed her mind. 'Let's go to the bar.'

'Sure, if that's what you want.' He inclined his head, making it seem he was accommodating her.

He really was the most aggravating man, Tory thought as they entered the hotel bar.

Large and well lit, it lacked intimacy but was almost empty. He installed her into a corner booth and was about to go and order at the counter when a waiter appeared. Lucas ordered a steak and salad, and insisted she have at least a sandwich.

From the bowing and scraping that went on, Tory assumed Lucas Ryecart was a familiar face.

'Big tipper, are we?' She couldn't resist remarking as the young waiter disappeared.

'Not especially,' he said with a grin, 'but Chuck is, so I guess I get the obsequious treatment through association.'

'Your magazine-buying friend,' she recalled out loud. 'He's staying here, too.'

'Was,' he confirmed. 'A bit too rural for him so he's moved back into the Ritz.'

In London, Tory assumed he meant. 'You make it sound as if he's living there.'

'He is for the moment,' he relayed, 'there and the New York Plaza. He commutes between the two.'

It seemed an odd way of life, even for a successful businessman. 'Has he a family?'

'He's between wives,' Lucas said, 'and has no children apart from a grown-up stepson... You're looking at him, by the way.'

Had she understood correctly?

'Chuck is your stepfather?'

'Is or was—I'm not sure which. He's remarried a couple of times since then.'

'Was, I think,' Tory volunteered, 'otherwise I'd have a multiplicity. Or two officials, anyway.'

Tory was normally reticent about her background but it seemed she'd met a fellow traveller, parent-wise.

'How old were you when your parents divorced?' His enquiry was matter-of-fact rather than sympathetic.

She answered in the same vein, 'They didn't. They were never married.'

He studied her face. 'You find that embarrassing?'

'No!' she claimed a little too sharply. 'Why should I?'

'No reason,' he mollified. 'It's hardly unusual these days... So were they the original pot-smoking hippies?'

Tory resented that question, too. 'Is that relevant to my work at Eastwich?'

'It might be,' he responded evenly, 'if you were to work with Alex on his drug story. It's best to go into these things with an open mind.'

Tory was tempted to argue with him, to say she was as objective as any good documentary-maker should be, but she wasn't sure if she were in this case. The truth was her mother had done drugs in the past. So-called soft drugs, but they had made Maura more feckless than ever. Tory had been old enough to know and disapprove, but too young to do much about it. It was one of the times she'd voluntarily decamped and returned to her grandparents in Purley.

'I would prefer to work on another story,' she declared at length.

'Fine by me,' he acknowledged with a brief smile. 'How convincing do you think you'd be as a features editor for a woman's magazine?'

For a split second Tory thought he was recommending she seek alternative employment, then she realised he was referring to the programme he'd proposed.

'You want me to do the *Toi/Vitalis* job?'

'Well—'

'Because I'm a woman?' That had been Simon's rationale.

'No, not especially,' Lucas Ryecart denied. 'I just can't envisage Alex trekking over moorland unless there's a pub at the end of the road and I don't see Simon in the role of observer, blending quietly into the background.'

Tory couldn't argue with either statement but was left feeling the job was hers through default.

'Right,' she murmured, her expression saying more.

'You're not happy?'

'Do I have to be?'

'Well, yes,' he countered. 'I don't want a good programme sabotaged by a lack of commitment on your part. So, if you're not up to this assignment, I'd sooner you say so now.'

And that's me told, Tory thought as she once more glimpsed a hard businessman behind the easygoing charmer.

The food arrived, giving her a moment or two to consider her response.

'I am up to it,' she claimed in a more positive manner. 'When do I start?'

She'd intended to sound keen but she wasn't prepared for his answer.

'This afternoon. You have an appointment with Personnel at the offices of *Toi*.'

'In London?'

He nodded.

'What if I don't get the job?'

He smiled at her naïvety.

'You already have. The interviews were last month. You've been a feature writer on a regional newspaper and this is your first magazine post.'

While he ran through her proposed cover, Tory suddenly realised what she was really taking on. She was going to have to lie about herself and her background and keep those lies consistent.

'Will anyone know I'm not a bona fide employee?'

'Only the personnel director of the group, and he's aware of your role.'

Tory wasn't altogether sure if she was.

'You don't expect me to provoke trouble?' she asked uncertainly.

'Absolutely not,' he said with emphasis. 'We want no charges of *manufacturing* material otherwise Eastwich's credibility will be blown. Sit back and observe like you did today.'

Tory couldn't help asking, 'Is that a criticism?'

'A comment,' he amended. 'After Alex and Simon's self-promotion, your reticence was almost refreshing although potentially limiting, careerwise… That's advice, by the way, not a threat.'

Tory nodded, accepting what he was saying. She had to push herself forward more.

She did so now, telling him, 'I do have ideas, you know.'

'I'm sure you do,' he responded. 'The trouble is, you let them be appropriated by other people.'

'We work as a team,' she stated a little testily.

'Yeah?' He raised a brow in disbelief. 'Perhaps someone should tell that to Alex and Simon. They seem to be playing on opposite sides. And your loyalty…well, we both know where that currently lies.'

With Alex, he meant, and Tory found herself colouring as if it were true. But it wasn't. Not in the sense he was implying.

'Alex is my boss. That's all!'

'So you keep saying.'

'Because it's true.'

'Okay, I'm your boss, too,' he reminded her unnecessarily. 'Can *I* come and share your flat?'

He gave her a mocking smile.

Tired of defending herself, Tory replied in the same vein. 'Sure. Why not? You could pull rank and pinch the sofa from Alex.'

Their eyes met and his smile faded. 'You're trying to say you're not sleeping with Alex?'

'No, I *am* saying that,' she corrected. 'Ask him, if you like.'

'Then why the pretence that Alex is living elsewhere?' he challenged.

'Because sometimes *other people* take two and two and make five,' she countered pointedly.

His eyes narrowed. '*Other people* have heard of Alex's reputation with women. I understand he's tested out more than one sofa since his wife left.'

Tory knew that was true enough so didn't comment. She said instead, 'Look, I like to keep home and work separate. And as far as work goes, Alex is my boss, plain and simple.'

It begged the question, 'And home?'

Tory felt she'd already answered it, and said flippantly, 'An extremely annoying flatmate who leaves the top off the toothpaste.'

He smiled briefly but disbelief lurked behind his eyes. Why could he not accept the truth?

Tory shook her head and, to her relief, he finally moved the conversation back to the magazine project, briefing her in what he saw as her role—passive but observant.

'When do I actually start work there?' Tory asked with some anticipation.

'Tomorrow,' he replied succinctly.

'*Tomorrow?*' She hadn't been expecting such short notice.

He nodded. 'That'll give you four days at the magazine before the team-bonding weekend.'

'But the magazine's in London,' she protested faintly.

'Which is where we're going now,' he added, 'or as soon as we've finished lunch and you've gone home to pack.'

Pack?

'You want me to stay over?' Tory was wide-eyed with suspicion.

'Is that a problem?'

He looked back at her, all innocence.

'In London?'

She wanted to make sure she'd understood.

'That's the general idea, yes.'

He nodded.

'With you?' She stared back stonily.

'If you like, although I hadn't planned on it,' he revealed. 'It's certainly an interesting proposition.'

'I w-wasn't...I didn't...I—I...' Tory stammered on until she saw the grin spreading on his face.

'No, I know.' He let her off the hook.

But he still laughed.

Damn the man.

CHAPTER SIX

Lucas Ryecart went on to explain. Tory had her appointment with the magazine at four p.m. and the plan was for her then to stay at a London hotel while she worked the rest of the week at *Toi*. At the same time he had a meeting with an investment banker and would be staying overnight at an entirely different hotel. Both venues were in central London so common sense dictated they travel down together. End of story.

Chastened, Tory accepted his offer of a lift and he trailed her back to her flat so she could pack a case. He waited outside for her.

They then travelled at speed towards the capital and Tory stared out at the motorway embankment rather than engage in further conversation. Having virtually accused him of luring her to the big city for immoral purposes, she felt silence was now her best option.

They'd reached the outskirts of London when her mobile rang.

Taking it out of her bag, she recognised the number calling as her office one. She pressed the receive button and wasn't too surprised to find it was Alex, wondering where she was. She didn't really get a chance to answer before he launched into a diatribe against the American, based on that morning's meeting.

Tory quickly switched the phone to her other ear, hoping Lucas hadn't caught the words 'arrogant ass' as Alex warmed to his theme. It seemed his enthusiasm for the American had dimmed somewhat.

She repeated Alex's name a couple of times in warning tones before actually cutting across him to say, 'Actually, Mr Ryecart's here beside me if you want to speak to him.'

79

It stopped Alex in his tracks momentarily, then he dropped volume as he proceeded to play twenty questions. Most she managed to field with 'yes's or 'no's and kept her voice carefully neutral.

To say Alex wasn't best pleased at her sudden secondment was an understatement and, in typical self-centred Alex fashion, he began to wonder how he was meant to get to work in the mornings, before he realised her car would still be in Norwich and was, therefore, available. She should have refused, of course. She didn't altogether trust Alex to drive it in a sane, sensible, sober fashion, but he pleaded and cajoled and called her Tory darling until she finally surrendered, more to shut him up than anything else.

When he finally hung up, she waited expectantly for comment from the American. She didn't have to wait long.

'So do you agree with him?' Lucas Ryecart drawled. 'Am I an arrogant ass?'

'You heard.'

'I'm not deaf.'

Tory supposed he would have to have been not to have caught Alex's initial remarks.

She tried bluffing. She was almost certain Alex hadn't used Lucas's name once.

'You're assuming that Alex was talking about you,' she muttered back.

He glanced from the road, fixing her with a sceptical look. 'Unless he happens to have a beef with another *swaggering Yank*. That's always possible, I suppose.'

Tory coloured as she realised he'd heard even more than she'd realised.

'Well, you know what they say about eavesdroppers,' she replied with some idea of putting him on the defensive.

'What?' He gave a short, mocking laugh. 'That they should immediately pull over onto the hard shoulder and climb out of the car while their passengers take abusive calls about them?'

This time Tory didn't argue back. He was right, of course. It was absurd to accuse him of eavesdropping when he could hardly have avoided listening to Alex's rant and rave.

She switched tacks. 'I'm sorry if you've taken offence but it's par for the course to bitch about your boss and you have put Alex's nose a little out of joint.'

She felt she'd laid on the right degree of humility but he made a dismissive sound.

'You think I care about Simpson's opinion? Believe me, I've been insulted by better men than him. The question was: do you agree with him?'

Tory was tempted to say, Yes, she did, but it seemed an act of extreme recklessness in their present situation.

She plumped for a circumspect, 'I have no thoughts on the subject.'

To which he muttered, 'Coward,' but in an amused rather than unpleasant tone. 'By the way, I wouldn't inform Simpson I'd overheard him.'

'Why not?' She would have imagined he'd want the opposite.

'A man in his position has only two ways to go,' he continued. 'He'll either feel the need to climb down and so embarrass us both with an apology I don't want and he won't mean. Or he'll be compelled to back up his remarks with a show of machismo for your benefit which, at the very least, will support my gut instinct that Simpson isn't worth the trouble he causes.'

'Right.' Tory saw the point he was making and the wisdom of it. 'I'll keep quiet.'

'Smart move,' he applauded her decision, then ran on, 'You know what really sticks in my craw about Simpson?'

Tory assumed it was a rhetoric question so didn't volunteer an answer.

Lucas continued, 'Forget the anti-American insults or his pompous posturing, the worst thing is the fact that he's just not good enough for a girl like you.'

Tory sighed loudly, wondering what she could say back to that. She was weary of denying involvement with Alex.

She said instead, 'And who do you imagine is?'

'Pretty much any personable, intelligent man without a drink problem would be an improvement,' he drawled back.

Not himself, then. Did that mean he'd lost interest? Tory supposed she should have been pleased but perhaps she was female enough to feel piqued as well.

She was considering her reply when he switched to saying, 'I'll leave that thought with you. Meanwhile, let's test your navigation skills. There's an A to Z in the glove compartment. We're looking for a Hermitage Road, NW something.'

'Okay.' Tory was glad of a change of subject and did as he suggested.

She didn't have to make much reference to the A to Z because she knew this part of London, and she guided him to the offices of the magazine without too much trouble.

'You're pretty good at giving directions,' he commented as they drew up outside the offices of *Toi*.

'For a woman, you mean?' Tory read the unspoken words in the compliment.

'I didn't say that,' he claimed even as a half-smile admitted it.

'I come from London,' Tory confessed, and, seeing she had five minutes to her appointment, began to collect her things together. 'Is the boot open?'

'Boot?' he repeated, then translated, 'The trunk?'

'Possibly,' she replied dryly. 'I need my case.'

'Won't it keep till I pick you up?'

'You're coming back for me?'

He nodded. 'Sure. I'll take you on to your hotel.'

'There's no need,' Tory dismissed quickly. 'I can get a taxi.'

'To where?'

'My hotel.'

'Which is?'

Tory frowned. What game were they playing now?

'You tell me,' she countered.

'I will when I find out,' he agreed. 'I've left Colin Mathieson's secretary to arrange it.'

'Right.' She should have known he wouldn't bother with any matter so trivial. 'I'll wait here for you, then.'

'I'll give you a call when I'm on my way,' he suggested. 'What's your cell-phone number?'

'I'll write it down.' She started to look in her bag for paper.

'That's okay,' he dismissed. 'Just tell me it.'

She did as he asked, and he repeated it as if it was already committed to memory.

Tory had her doubts. She certainly couldn't memorise an eleven-digit number after one hearing. But who knew what this man could do?

'I'd better go.' She glanced at her watch again. 'I don't want to be late for my interview.'

'Good luck, then.'

'I thought the job was mine.'

'It is,' he assured. 'That's the easy part.'

Tory supposed he was right. Convincing the rest of the magazine staff that she was a bona fide features editor might prove more difficult.

She finally climbed out of the car and walked up the steps of the magazine office, conscious that Lucas had yet to drive away. She turned round and he saluted her briefly. She didn't wave back but went ahead through the revolving doors that opened out into a reception.

'Yes.' An elegant blonde looked her up and down from behind a desk.

Tory said her name and she noticed the blonde's eyes flicker with recognition but no warmth before she was asked to take a seat in Reception.

She'd barely sat and picked up this month's edition of *Toi* when another identikit blonde arrived to escort her upstairs to the personnel director's office.

The interview was, as Lucas had said, just a formality, but she sensed the director wasn't altogether enthusiastic about her reason for being there. He used the expression 'the powers that be' when he referred to the magazine's new owner, Chuck Wiseman, and just stopped short of calling the team-bonding weekend psychological claptrap. He also warned her that, due to the unusual circumstances surrounding her hiring, she might possibly encounter some hostility from the editorial staff.

'I'm not sure I understand,' she queried this statement. 'Do you mean some know why I'm here?'

'Not that, no,' the personnel director assured her. 'If they did, we might have a walk-out on our hands. In fact, I have warned the *powers that be* of just such a consequence if you are discovered.'

'Then why should they be hostile?' she pursued.

'I'm only speculating on the possibility,' he backtracked a little. 'After all, there were at least two junior editors who felt they were in line for your post plus the fact it was never advertised. To all intents and purposes, you appear to have been given the job purely on personal recommendation from, let's say, above.'

'I see.' Tory did, too. She was joining a woman's magazine—a notoriously bitchy work environment, anyway—already viewed as someone's protégé. 'Who do they imagine has imposed me?'

'There are various theories,' he hedged, 'which I won't go into. I just feel you should be warned that you may get a somewhat frosty reaction.'

'Thanks.' Tory pulled a face.

She sensed he wasn't in the least bit sympathetic. Someone had obviously ridden roughshod over him, too.

'I'm afraid there isn't much I can do to improve the situation,' he added in the same cool tones.

'Don't worry, I'll survive.' Tory was sure she would.

The mishmash of types found on a woman's magazine was hardly as scary as some of the loud-mouthed, disaffected girls with whom she'd gone to school. At least no one here was likely to threaten to beat her up for her lunch money.

'I'm glad you're so confident.' He clearly didn't share the feeling. 'Anyway, I'll show you round the editorial department.'

She followed him to the lifts and they went back down to the editorial floor which was largely open plan. Tory trailed in his wake, conscious of curious eyes on her.

They stopped at a closed office at the end and Tory was introduced to Amanda Villiers, the editor-in-chief, who was currently conducting a meeting with several staff.

If she hadn't been pre-warned, Tory would not have understood Amanda Villiers's attitude. While on the surface her new boss was all polite handshake and smiles, there was an edge to every remark she made.

'I read your résumé with interest,' she drawled. '*The Cornpickers Times*, that was your first job, wasn't it? Features editor of the women's page.'

'*Cornwall Times*,' Tory corrected, while knowing the mistake had been deliberate.

Amanda was playing to an audience and several of her staff had dutifully tittered at her remark.

'Whatever.' Amanda Villiers smiled tightly. 'I didn't come up the provincial route. What does one write about for farmers' wives? How to get sheep dye from under their fingernails? Or how to prepare the perfect *Boeuf en Croute*—after one's killed it first, of course.'

Tory laughed, having some idea she wasn't meant to, and Amanda looked a little surprised.

'You've forgotten knit yourself a designer sweater, using your own flock,' suggested Tory on the same theme and took the wind out of Amanda's sails.

'Yes, well, all very fascinating, I'm sure,' Amanda said with a dismissive air, 'but a national women's magazine is, of course, a whole different world. Not that I need to tell you that. You did two years on that French magazine…what's it called again?'

Good question. Tory had spent an hour of the car journey that afternoon memorising her CV but it evidently hadn't been long enough.

'I don't imagine anyone's heard of it,' she murmured evasively.

'No, I certainly hadn't—' Amanda sniffed '—but, do tell, darling, how does one go from the *Cornish Times* to some sub-porno in Paris?'

Tory considered declaring herself not the type of person to work on a sub-porno, but she was already having enough trouble building any credibility without discussing ethics.

'It's a long story,' she told the room at large, 'with which

I may bore everyone when we're lying in our sleeping bags listening to the wind whistling round our tents.'

'Oh, God, the adventure weekend.' Amanda groaned aloud. 'You know about it and you still want to work here? You must be desperate.'

'I'm sure the job will make up for it.' Tory forced some enthusiasm into her voice.

Amanda looked sceptical and turned to a younger woman on her right. 'What do you think, Sam? You've been doing the job for the last six months. Is it worth a weekend in some godforsaken spot in the dales?'

Sam, a woman of about thirty, glanced between her boss, Amanda, and Tory, before making some inaudible comment, then staring rigidly at the notepad in front of her.

The set of her shoulders betrayed anger barely held in check. The only question was, where was this anger directed: at Tory who'd prevented her from being promoted, or the taunting Amanda whom Tory herself already felt like pushing off a cliff, given half a chance?

'Anyway, I'd better introduce you round.' Amanda finally remembered her manners and rattled off names and job titles too quickly for Tory to assimilate. 'When do you start?'

'As soon as possible,' Tory replied briefly.

'In that case, grab a pew,' Amanda suggested and left Tory with little choice.

She couldn't count on rescue from the personnel director because he was on his way out, problem disposed of.

Still, what happened next was familiar territory after that morning. While Amanda conducted a brainstorming session on cosmetic surgery, Tory was once again made to feel part of the furniture. Ideas were thrown up for discussion, opinions sought, criticisms levied but no one sought to include Tory in any of it.

This was not altogether surprising as the rest took their lead from Amanda and, having humiliated Tory sufficiently for the moment, the editor now ignored her totally.

Just as well, Tory realised, because she had little positive to say on the subject of breast implants or liposuction. She accepted some women felt the need for self-improvement but it seemed a growing obsession, the quest for the body beautiful. Magazines were full of such articles and the only question was whether they were documenting or feeding the phenomenon.

'What about you, Victoria?' Amanda finally addressed her. 'Have you had any fine tuning? Boob job, perhaps?' She glanced towards Tory's moderately sized chest, before deciding, 'No, maybe not... That nose, however. Very retroussé. What do you think, girls?'

Two of the women laughed as if she'd said something witty but a young woman at the end of the table seemed to suppress a sigh.

It made Tory wonder just what hidden tensions would be exposed after so many unrelieved hours in each other's company over the weekend.

For herself, she was already glad she worked for Eastwich and Alex for all his faults rather than the autocratic Amanda.

When Tory's cell-phone interrupted the meeting, Amanda gave her a look of pity before drawling, 'A golden rule, darling, mobiles off during meetings. I thought you'd have known that.'

Tory grimaced—as far as she was going to get to apology— and read the number calling. It was another mobile. She guessed it was Lucas.

'Who is it?' Amanda asked impatiently.

'A friend, he's giving me a lift,' Tory explained.

'Man friend?'

'Yes.'

'Lucky you.'

Amanda actually sounded more sincere than usual but Tory waited for the punchline. When it didn't come, she offered, 'I'll ask him to call back later.'

'No, don't bother. Time to wrap up, don't you think, *mes enfants*?'

The others nodded and Tory wondered if any ever disagreed with Amanda. Perhaps any who had were long gone.

'Well, answer him,' Amanda instructed, 'before he gives you up for dead.'

'All right… Hi,' she said into the mouthpiece.

Lucas replied simply, 'I'm outside.'

'Okay, be there in a moment,' she promised and rang off.

'Masterful type, is he?' Amanda concluded from this brief exchange.

'You could say that.' Tory nodded back.

'Love those, myself,' Amanda commented, 'in bed, at any rate. Not so keen when they're strutting about, demanding their socks washed and their breakfast cooked.'

Tory forced a laugh and wondered briefly if it was in the job description—to laugh at Amanda's jokes.

'Well, run along, mustn't keep him waiting, Vicki, darling,' the older woman urged in mocking tones that had Tory gritting her teeth.

But she did as she was told, anxious to get away from Amanda and her coven.

Fortunately she remembered her way back to the lift because no one volunteered to escort her, although she did find herself waiting with one of the other sub-editors. She recognised the girl who went in for sighing rather than sniggering.

'So what's your opinion?' the girl asked as they descended in the lift together. 'Think you'll like it here?'

Tory shrugged. 'Early days.'

'She doesn't get any better,' the girl drawled back, 'and she seems to have developed a pretty instant dislike of you, if you don't mind me saying so.'

Tory actually did mind, especially as it reinforced her own suspicions that working for Amanda was going to be a nightmare. Thank God, it was only temporary.

'I'll live with it,' Tory said at length.

Her lift companion regarded her with a look that seemed to waiver between pitying and admiring before the doors slid open and they parted in the reception area.

Tory didn't hang around. In fact, she almost ran down the steps to Lucas's awaiting car.

'How was it?' he said as she climbed into the passenger seat.

She released a breath of pent-up anger, before responding, 'Don't ask!'

'That bad?' he concluded.

'Worse.' Tory shuddered even before she spotted Amanda emerging from the building.

He followed her gaze. 'Who's that?'

'The editor from hell.' She grimaced. 'Can we go?'

'Yeah, sure,' he agreed easily and, putting the car in gear, drove towards the exit. 'I take it you were introduced.'

'More than introduced,' she relayed. 'After the briefest of inductions, the personnel director abandoned me to the pack.'

'The pack?'

'Editorial staff,' she qualified, 'but, believe me, the lions of the Serengeti would definitely seem friendlier.'

He laughed, then saw from her face she wasn't really joking. 'You don't think your cover was already blown.'

She shook her head. 'More a case of noses out of joint. Apparently one of them has been Acting Features Editor for months so she's hardly overjoyed by my appearance and, as for the editor-in-chief, Amanda Villiers, she resents having some nobody from nowhere imposed on them through suspect channels.'

'Well, never mind,' he tried to console, 'you only have to put up with it for a few days.'

'It's going to seem like weeks,' she complained. 'Forget their open hostility, have you ever tried pretending to be someone you're not?'

'Actually, yes,' he replied. 'I once passed myself off as the deaf and dumb son of a goat-herder in Northern Afghanistan.'

'Is that a joke?' The amused note in his voice certainly suggested it was.

'Not particularly, although it had its humorous moments,' he confided, before explaining, 'I was covering the Russian/Afghani conflict when I ended up in a situation where being an American journalist wasn't good for the health... Mind you, neither's going without food for a couple of days, but I survived,' he finished with a dry laugh.

Tory realised it was a true story. She had forgotten his former life as a foreign correspondent. This was the first he'd alluded to it.

'All right, you win.' She picked up the not-so-hidden message. 'I admit working undercover at *Toi* hardly rates in the danger stakes, but I'm still nervous about blowing it. I mean, I only know in the vaguest of terms what a features editor does. I'm going to be as hopeless as they think I am.'

Lucas pondered the last remark before pointing out, 'But if they're expecting you to mess up, it won't matter if you do, will it?'

'I suppose not,' Tory agreed. 'I just don't want to give Amanda Villiers the satisfaction.'

'Yeah, I've heard she's pretty monstrous.'

'You've heard? From whom?'

'Chuck. At least, I'm guessing it's the same woman. He calls her Mandy.'

'To her face?' Tory didn't think that would go down well.

'I guess so.' Lucas nodded. 'He took her out for lunch once and I don't see Chuck calling her Miss Villiers.'

'A business lunch, you mean?' pursued Tory.

He shrugged. 'Could have been... Is she pretty?'

Tory blinked at the question, before saying, 'Possibly. That was her on the steps.'

'Maybe not business, then,' he judged. 'Chuck certainly has an eye for a pretty lady.'

Tory glanced in his direction and saw the smile slanting his lips. It seemed he admired his stepfather for this.

'Isn't he...well, isn't he...?' She found no tactful way to express her doubts.

He did it for her, saying, 'Too old? Yeah, probably. But women don't seem to mind that. Chuck has a lot of charm. A lot of money, too,' he added dryly.

'And it doesn't bother you?' Tory couldn't resist asking.

He thought about it for a moment, then shrugged. 'Chuck's smart enough to look out for himself.'

It didn't really answer her question. 'But what about your mother? Does she still care?'

He shook his head. 'Mom's been dead twenty years.'

'I'm sorry,' she said automatically.

He gave her a quizzical look. 'What for?'

'Being nosy, I suppose.'

'Don't worry about it. I took it as a good sign.'

'Sign?' She was wary once more.

'That you're at least interested enough in me to ask such personal questions,' he stated, a smile in his voice.

Tory just stopped herself from saying, Don't flatter yourself, and responded instead, 'I was making conversation. That's all.'

'Yeah, okay.' He made a pacifying gesture with his hand. 'But for the record I am a forty-one-year-old widower. Both parents dead. No dependants. Sane. Healthy. Solvent. No unusual vices.'

His autobiography sounded so like a personal ad, Tory pointed out, 'You missed out with G.S.O.H. and W.L.T.M. young, attractive female for fun relationship.'

It drew a laugh before he drawled back, 'I find people who claim to have a good sense of humour often don't, and I've already met the young attractive female, thanks very much, although I'm not sure she goes in for "fun relationships".'

He meant her, of course. At least, Tory assumed he did. But she could hardly know for certain unless she asked him and that seemed a very unwise thing to do.

Her glance found him wearing the amused expression that was pretty much a fixture on his face.

'No comment?' he prompted.

Tory gritted her teeth, 'I doubt she's *your* type, then.'

'We'll have to see,' he replied, smile still in place. 'Meanwhile, let's get you settled in your hotel. It's called The Balmoral, Kingscote Avenue and is somewhere in W10.'

Tory picked up the A to Z once more and located their current position. Finding the hotel was something else. For all its grand name it was tucked away in a back street of a rather down-at-heel part of Earl's Court.

Not that she was about to raise any objections. She'd lived in worse areas with her mother and, although the hotel looked down-market, too, Eastwich's budget didn't usually stretch to much better.

It was Lucas Ryecart who said, 'Don't bother getting out,' when she made a move to do so. 'You're not staying in this dump.'

'It's probably nicer inside.'

'It would have to be.' He pulled a face. 'See that guy who's just walked into the joint? Russian Mafia, I'd say, if I didn't think they could afford better.'

Tory had seen the gentleman. Leather-coated with an up-turned collar, he'd had a lean, mean unshaven face and sus-picious air, but was probably an innocent foreign tourist.

'Well, if he is,' she suggested, 'think of the story I could write for *Toi*: Russian Mafia plan gold bullion robbery from royally named hotel. That would give the magazine much-needed edge, at any rate.'

'May I remind you, you work for Eastwich, not *Toi*?' he threw back. 'And that if you write bad things about the Mafia, they don't settle for complaining to the Press Complaints Commission. Let's go.'

'Where?' she asked as he pulled away.

'You can have my room tonight,' he replied and, anticipat-ing any objection, added, '*Have*, I said, not *share*.'

'What will you do?' Tory was still not convinced by the assurance.

'Don't worry about me,' he dismissed. 'I'm having dinner with a friend who can probably put me up for the night.'

Friend? Male or female? The question crept into Tory's head, and, when she opted for the answer female, she felt a pang of jealousy, pure and simple. But why? She didn't want to get involved with him, did she?

Every shred of sense said no, but that didn't diminish her attraction to him. It wasn't merely his looks. The sound of his voice stirred something in her, too, and the way he moved, and his directness, though it was often disconcerting.

'In fact,' he resumed, 'when I come to think of it, this friend could probably help you—or, at least, his wife might.'

His wife. A moment's relief was quickly followed by denial. She hadn't really been concerned, had she?

'In what way?' she queried.

'She used to work for a woman's glossy before the kids came along,' he explained. 'She could give you the low-down on what a features editor does on a day-to-day basis.'

'That would certainly be useful.' Tory seriously doubted her ability to bluff through four working days before the adventure weekend.

'Okay, come to dinner, and you can pick her brains.' It was a fairly casual invitation.

Tory still hesitated. 'Won't they mind—you turning up with a total stranger?'

'Why should they?' He shrugged. 'Unless you become a major embarrassment after a glass or two of wine.'

'Not as far as I know,' she stated heavily.

'That's all right, then,' he replied, and, turning into the parking space in front of one of the biggest hotels in London, announced, 'We're here.'

A doorman appeared to open the passenger door while Lucas climbed out and opened the boot. He indicated her case and his overnight bag to the hovering porter before handing over his car keys so the vehicle could be parked somewhere.

'I'm going to leave the car here,' he explained as they went through the revolving door into the lobby, 'and retrieve it in the morning rather than search South Kensington for a parking space.'

She nodded at this information but wondered why he'd let the porter take his bag. Did he imagine she could be persuaded to let him share the room? If so, he was in for a disappointment.

'Reservation in the name of Ryecart,' he announced as they approached the desk, and, when it was located, informed them, 'A Miss Lloyd will actually be using the room. Is it possible to extend the booking from one night to four?'

Four nights? Did he mean for her? It seemed so.

When he'd finished business with the desk clerk, he said, 'You might as well stay here for the duration. Save the bother of finding somewhere else.'

'But surely it's too…' She pulled a face rather than say the word expensive in front of the porter.

'It's on Eastwich,' he said as if that made the money irrelevant.

She supposed it was his decision. After all, he *was* Eastwich in a sense. But hadn't he been griping about budgets to Alex just that morning?

Lucas checked his luggage into the porter's office to be picked up later. 'Why don't you freshen up before we go to my friends for dinner?' he suggested to Tory. 'Take your time. I have some calls to make, then I'll wait in the cocktail bar.'

Tory didn't actually remember agreeing to this dinner date, but wasn't given much chance to object as he turned on his heel and walked off towards the hotel lounges. She was left in the care of the porter who guided her to her room on the fifth floor.

The room was every bit as luxurious as she'd expected and, after the porter had departed, tip in hand, she spent a little while looking across the London skyline. Then, still debating the wisdom of going with Lucas on any date, however innocuous it seemed, she showered, changed into a pale lilac shift dress and spent at least twenty minutes trying to sweep her unruly hair into a sophisticated style before giving up and letting it fall back into a mass of curls.

It wasn't a proper date, of course. It was more in the nature of work. That was what she told herself, even as she checked once more how she looked in the mirror, before draping a cream pashmina round her arms and venturing out to find him.

As it was early evening, the cocktail lounge wasn't crowded. From the doorway Tory noticed him at the bar, talking to a stunning brunette of supermodel proportions. She was considering retreat when he spotted her in turn. He made some final remark to the brunette before crossing to greet Tory.

He noted her change of outfit with a smiling, 'You look lovely.'

Tory replied with a less gracious, 'Humph,' and followed it up by muttering, 'We can pass on dinner, if you prefer.'

'And do what?' He arched an interested brow.

He'd misunderstood so Tory glanced pointedly towards the brunette. 'You could pursue new interests.'

He followed her gaze, then laughed dryly as he curled a hand round Tory's elbow to guide her to the front lobby.

'You're not jealous, are you?' he added in amused tones.

She gave him a repressive glance, claiming, 'Not even remotely.'

'Shame.' He pulled a doleful face. 'No need, anyway. Pros like her don't do it for me.'

Tory assumed he meant professional women and threw back, 'Too challenging, are they? Women in executive positions?'

He looked puzzled for a moment, then gave another laugh. 'I think we may have lost something in the translation. When I say "pro", I mean, well, to put it politely, a lady of the night.'

'Lady of the...' The penny finally dropped with Tory and left her round-eyed with disbelief. 'That girl...she was...no, she couldn't be.'

He nodded before switching subjects to say, 'I'll need your room key.'

'What for?' she queried.

'My overnight bag,' he reminded her slowly and indicated the porter's lodge tucked into a corner of the lobby. 'They'll have it stored under room number.'

'Oh.' She just had to stop reacting with suspicion to everything he said. 'Here.'

She produced it out of her clutch purse and waited while he retrieved his case.

They emerged from the hotel to find it still light and sunny on this summer's evening.

The liveried doorman assumed they'd want a taxi and was already signalling for one from the rank alongside the entrance.

Once they were installed in the back, curiosity had Tory resuming their earlier conversation. 'Did she ask you for money, then? The woman in the bar.'

'Not up front,' he told her. 'She'd be thrown out of the hotel if she went around doing that.'

'Then how did you know?' she pursued.

He smiled a little as he asked, 'Do you think I'm irresistible?'

'No!'

'Well, neither do I. So, when some stunning-looking dame comes up to me in a bar, sits down, uninvited, and asks me if I'm in need of company, I can guess everything's not quite on the level.'

'She *might* just have fancied you,' Tory argued. 'You're not that bad-looking.'

'Gee, thanks,' he said at this grudging admission, 'but, no, I don't think it was love at first sight.'

'What else did she say?'

'She asked me if I was in London on business. She then said she was *doing business*, should I be interested. I told her I was waiting for a friend and she was just offering to find a friend for my friend when you came to my rescue,' he finished in wry tones.

Tory made a slight face. This man didn't need her help to get out of such a situation. He was obviously a man of the world.

'You weren't tempted,' she challenged, 'stunning as she was?'

'Not even remotely,' he echoed her earlier words. 'Paying to have a woman tell me how great I am in bed has never held appeal.'

Tory felt herself actually blushing.

And that was before he leaned closer to murmur, 'Eliciting such information for real, now, that's a different matter.'

For once there was no amusement in his low deep drawl. It was Tory who forced a laugh.

'You don't believe I can?' he added. 'Or was that an invitation to prove it?'

It hadn't been, of course, but he still lifted a hand to her cheek and, when she didn't immediately pull away, turned her face towards his.

He stared at her so long Tory assumed that was all he was going to do. Then he kissed her. Not deeply or intimately. His lips barely touched against the corner of her mouth while a hand lightly pushed back the curls framing her face.

It was over almost before it was begun. He drew away and leaned back against the taxi leather.

Tory was left confused and somewhat irrationally annoyed. If he was going to kiss her, he should do it properly or not at all.

'An ominous silence followed,' he commented as if writing a novel, 'but still he counted himself lucky—at least she hadn't slapped him.'

'Yet,' Tory warned darkly.

But too late. A quick glance confirmed that the amused smile was back in place.

'I'm not sure I want to go to dinner with you,' she added in haughty tones.

'Well, it's too late for a rain check,' he countered. 'We're here.'

Here being a splendid row of Georgian terraced houses. Rich friends, obviously.

'Do they know I'm coming too?' she asked as he selected cash from his wallet to pay the taxi.

He nodded and, paying the driver, helped her out of the taxi before answering, 'Caro does, anyway. In fact, she's looking forward to giving you the low-down on being a features editor. A trip down memory lane, she called it.'

'What does she do now?'

'Stays at home with the children.'

'How old?'

'The twins are about three, the baby is just a few months old... You like children?' he added as they walked up the steps.

'Boiled or fried?' she quipped.

He smiled at the small joke before pursuing, 'Seriously?'

'I like them well enough,' she finally replied. 'Just as long as I can hand them back.'

'I used to feel like that, too,' he agreed. 'Then one day you find yourself thinking it wouldn't be so bad, having your own.'

The admission was unexpected, so much so that Tory stared at him, testing if he was quite serious.

'With the right person, of course.' Blue eyes met hers, half intent, half amused.

Flirting, that was what he was doing. Tory knew that. Yet it seemed important to make a statement.

'I'll never have children.' She was unequivocal about it.

He smiled a little. 'How can you be so certain?'

Tory did not smile back. He obviously thought she was making a lifestyle choice.

'I just am.' She didn't feel like going into reasons.

She had told him. That was enough.

He shook his head, as if he still didn't believe her.

His problem, she decided.

It was only later she wished she'd told him it all.

CHAPTER SEVEN

LUCAS studied Tory for a moment longer, then said, 'You'll see, one day,' before turning to press on the doorbell.

It was answered by a woman wearing a frog apron on top of a smart summer dress. She was slightly older than Tory with a pretty freckled face and red hair escaping from a band at the neck. She looked a little flustered but her face was transformed at the sight of Lucas.

'Luc, lovely to see you.' She gave him a hug and a kiss on the cheek before turning to Tory. 'And you must be the features editor to be. Pleased to meet you. Come through, but mind the toys.'

She led the way down a wide hall, which was strewn with the pieces of a wooden train set, calling out, 'Boys, Uncle Luc is here.'

The effect was immediate as two identical pyjama-clad figures came hurtling out of a room to throw themselves at Lucas Ryecart's legs. Without hesitation, he stooped down and heaved one up in each arm, much to the boys' delight.

'Play trains,' demanded one.

'Build a tent,' demanded the other.

'Pillow fight!' added the first.

'Do the swingy thing,' chimed the second.

And so it went on as the twins began to list endless possibilities now opened up to them at the appearance of 'Uncle Luc'.

'*Boys!*' their mother eventually called over the excited gabbling. 'Uncle Luc is having dinner. *You* are going to bed.'

This elicited a joint protest of 'Aw' and crestfallen little faces.

'You heard your mother.' Lucas put them both back on the ground. 'But if you're up those stairs by the time I count five,

I may just tell you the really scary thing that happened to my friends, Al and Bill, the time they got lost in a jungle in South America.'

'A real jungle?'

'Honestly?'

The boys' eyes were round with anticipation before Lucas began, 'One…two…'

Then there was a mad scramble as the two made for the stairs and rushed up as quickly as their legs would allow.

'You don't have to,' Caro said as he reached five.

'I'd like to.' He raised a brow in Tory's direction. 'You don't mind?'

Tory shook her head. Caro seemed friendly enough.

'It'll give us a chance to have a girl talk.' Caro grinned wickedly.

'About magazine work, I hope,' Lucas added.

'Of course. What else?' Caro feigned innocence, even as the gleam in her eye suggested he would also be a topic under discussion.

Then one of the twins appeared at the top of the stairs to shout, 'Is it five yet?'

'Shh, the baby's asleep!' his mother called back.

While Lucas promised, 'I'm coming, Jack,' and took the stairs two at a time.

'I don't know how he does it—' Caro gazed after him in puzzled admiration '—but he always gets their names right. Not even their grandmothers can do that.'

Tory wouldn't have managed it either. The boys had looked like clones of each other. 'Does he see them often?'

'He tries to—' Caro pulled a forgiving face '—but he has such a busy schedule. Still, the boys always love it when Uncle Luc comes. He's their godfather.'

'Really?' Tory assumed that was why he was called 'Uncle Luc'.

'Well, one of them,' Caro continued before glancing towards the back of the house. 'Look, do you mind if we chat in the kitchen while I get on with dinner?'

Tory shook her head, offering, 'I'd be happy to help. I'm

not much of a cook but I can peel vegetables with the best of them.'

'It's all right.' Carol smiled, leading the way through. 'Most of it's done. I just have to keep watch over various pots and pans. Poached salmon—I hope you like it.'

'Sounds delicious.' Tory meant it. 'A welcome change from chicken salad or tuna pasta, the heights of my own culinary achievements.'

Caro laughed. 'Oh, you're definitely one up on me. I used to live on a diet of sandwiches and yoghurt in my single career-girl days. Life always seemed too short to cook.'

'Quite.' Tory gave the other woman a complicit smile.

'Of course, it's such an irony,' Caro ran on. 'There I was, doing features for this lifestyle magazine, full of cordon bleu recipes and articles on minimalist decor, and going home to cook beans on toast in a girl-sharing flat in Clapham with enough clutter to fill a builder's skip.'

Tory laughed at the image, before casting an appreciative glance round her present surrounds. The kitchen was large and light and airy, with up to date units and flooring in polished beech-wood.

'You have a lovely place now,' complimented Tory.

'Money,' Caro replied as she stirred a simmering pot. 'My husband's family have it.'

'Right.' Tory wasn't sure how to respond to such frankness.

Caro shrugged, dismissing it as an importance, before continuing, 'Anyway, I understand from Luc that you're also about to enter the bitch-eat-bitch world of the women's glossy.'

'I've already been through the initiation ceremony.' Grimacing, Tory relayed her brief meeting with the editorial board.

Caro's expression was sympathetic but hardly surprised. It seemed Amanda Villiers, the senior editor, was notorious in the business for savaging female staff.

Tory listened while Caro went through what her job had entailed when working for a very similar magazine to *Toi*. Obviously she couldn't teach Tory how to do the job. That required years of experience as well as talent. But she gave her enough pointers on how to *seem* to be doing the job to maintain her cover for a few days.

'You'll be fine,' Caro tried to boost Tory's flagging confidence, 'but if you do need advice, I'm available, nappy-changing permitting.'

There was a certain wistfulness in her voice that made Tory ask, 'When did you stop work?'

'The boys were about two, I think…' Caro cast her mind back '…so that's…what? Over a year ago. I was one of those having-it-all-mothers who suddenly woke up to the fact they were really having-absolutely-nothing but misery and stress.'

Tory gave an understanding murmur. 'It seems to be a trend—women re-evaluating their lives. Personally, I love my work but I don't think I could manage it all—home, family and a career.'

'You can for a while,' Caro responded, 'but then your energy levels go down while theirs go up and all of a sudden the crying babies became talkative two-year-olds well able to tell you they hate it every time you leave for work and your nanny informs you she wants to see the world, starting tomorrow, and your heart is desperate for another baby even though you're barely coping with the two you have. So it's crunch time…I was luckier than most, I suppose, because we didn't need my money.'

'Still, you must miss work,' Tory said in sympathetic tones.

'At times,' Caro admitted, shaking the contents of a pan, 'when the twins' squabbling reaches an all-time high—or possibly low—and the baby won't settle because she has a cold and the au pair has failed to return from a night out clubbing.'

'And total strangers turn up for dinner?' Tory suggested, her tone apologetic.

'Oh, I didn't mind that.'

'Really?'

'Well—' Caro pulled a face '—I wasn't too ecstatic when Luc called, but that's only because I thought you might be like his usual girlfriends—'

'I'm not his girlfriend.' A frown clouded Tory's features. 'Did he say—?'

'No, not at all,' Caro was quick to disclaim. 'Quite the opposite, in fact...'

Caro trailed off and left Tory wondering what Lucas had said about her that was quite the opposite of being his girlfriend.

'I just meant,' Caro tried again, 'that, on the few occasions Lucas has brought a woman to dinner, it has been a girlfriend and they tend to be...let's say, a certain type.'

Tory told herself she wasn't interested but, in the very next breath, asked, 'What type, exactly?'

Caro hesitated. 'Perhaps I've said enough.'

'All right.' Tory wasn't going to press her.

That was probably why Caro ran on, 'Well, it could be me, but I find them all unbearably superior. Admittedly, they're usually barristers or investment bankers or run their own PR companies and they're always clever and witty, and often fairly stunning in the looks department, too. Which is probably why they feel obliged to talk down to lesser mortals, as if we're one step up from the village idiot.'

Tory rolled her eyes in agreement. 'I know the type but I can't imagine they talk to Lucas that way.'

'Oh, goodness, no!' Caro exclaimed at the very idea. 'But that only makes it worse. They positively simper in Luc's presence, and gaze at him, all adoring eyes, like politicians' wives.'

Tory laughed as intended, before venturing, 'He probably loves it.'

Caro looked uncertain. 'Luc's never struck me as being that big an egotist,' she replied, 'although I suppose most men that gorgeous *do* have egos the size of a planet.'

'Too true,' Tory said with feeling.

Caro came back with, 'So you think he is, then?'

'What?'

'Gorgeous.'

Caro's grin made a joke of it.

Tory pulled a slight face, too. 'I didn't say that, exactly.'

'No, but he is,' Caro insisted as if it were a fact that couldn't be disputed.

Tory didn't try; she was acquainted with the phrase 'the lady doth protest too much'.

'I have wondered if it's a kind of protection,' the other woman continued in musing tones.

'Protection?' Tory had lost the thread. 'What is?'

'Going out with that kind of woman,' Caro volunteered. 'I mean, even allowing for other people's taste, no one, but no one, could have found his last girlfriend lovable. Smart, witty, classy, yes! Lovable, absolutely not.'

'What happened to her?'

'His relocation to Norwich, but I can't see that being an insurmountable problem. How far is it from London? Two hours?'

Having made the journey that day, Tory said, 'A little over.'

'No huge distance,' commented Caro, 'but that's the excuse he gave for the relationship petering out. I wondered if he'd met someone else. Any super-intelligent, arrogant, super-model types at Eastwich?'

'Not that I can think of.' Tory certainly didn't come into that category. At five-foot six, she was hardly a super-model type, was far from super-intelligent, and didn't see herself as arrogant in personality. That left her questioning whether Lucas Ryecart was stringing along some other woman besides herself.

'At any rate,' Caro resumed her original theme, 'I have this theory he dates women with whom he's in no danger of falling in love. As in, it's better *not* to love and *not* to lose, than ever love at all.'

'I always thought it was the other way round,' countered Tory.

'It is,' replied Caro, 'but, in Luc's case, he *has* loved and lost so maybe he doesn't want to go through it again.'

'I see.' Tory did see, too; she just wasn't entirely convinced.

Sensing her doubts, Caro confided in more sober tones, 'He was married once and she died.'

'Yes, I know.'

'Did he tell you?'

Tory nodded, recalling he had told her at one point.

Caro looked surprised. 'He doesn't usually talk about it— even among the family.'

The family? Tory didn't quite follow. Which family did she mean?

'Is Lucas related to you?' she finally asked Caro.

'Sort of. His wife was my sister-in-law. Or would have been, had she...' The other woman tailed off at Tory's expression and switched to asking, 'Is something wrong?'

Tory struggled to keep her emotions in check as the truth dawned. Lucas was an only child, while his late wife had one brother. There was no other link.

How could she have been so stupid? *Uncle Luc* really was Uncle Luc. She was in Charlie's, her ex-fiancé's, house. She was talking to Charlie's wife, the girl who had so rapidly re-placed her.

'You really don't look well.' Caro watched Tory's face be-come drawn with alarm.

'I... It's a bug,' Tory lied desperately. 'I thought I was better, but it seems not. I'll have to go back to the hotel.'

Tory picked up the pashmina she'd draped over a chair and her handbag, and started making for the door.

Caro followed. 'Yes, of course, I'll go and fetch Luc. He'll—'

'No!' Tory refused rather abruptly, then softened it with, 'Honestly, I don't want to drag him away. I can hail a taxi. I'm sorry to throw out your plans. It was lovely to meet you...'

Tory garbled on until she was in the front hall, poised for escape.

Caro obviously didn't feel she should be allowed to go on her own and looked relieved at the sound of a key in the front door.

'That'll be Charlie now. I could get him to run you back instead.'

Tory said nothing, did nothing. She felt trapped, caught like a rabbit in headlights. She watched the door push open. Her eyes went to the dark-suited man entering.

For a moment she almost thought she'd got it wrong and this wasn't Charlie. He wasn't as she remembered. Five years older, he had lost some of his boyish good looks and his hair. Her heart was beating hard out of panic but it didn't kick up any extra gears, even when she realised it was most definitely Charlie.

His glance first went to his wife, who'd launched into explanations of their guest's indisposition, before it encompassed Tory. Then any hopes that she'd also changed out of recognition faded rapidly.

Charlie was clearly shocked, opening and shutting his mouth as no words came, struggling to come to terms with her presence.

When Caro sought to introduce them, 'This is Tory, by the way,' he was already mouthing the name he'd known her by: Vicki.

Quickly, she shook her head at him, the slightest movement, but he picked it up.

When she said, 'Pleased to meet you,' he followed suit.

'Yes, hello,' he murmured, and let her continue.

'I'm sorry, but I have to go. I'm not feeling too great and I've left my medicine back at the hotel.'

She waited for him to play his part, say some farewell words, encourage her to leave, perhaps open the door, but he just stood stock-still staring at her.

It was Caro who insisted, 'Charlie will run you back. Won't you, Charlie?'

She seemed oblivious of undercurrents.

Tory anticipated Charlie making an excuse and was thrown by his acquiescent, 'Yes, of course. My car's outside.'

'See.' Caro was finally satisfied with the arrangements.

She escorted Tory down the steps while Charlie went ahead to unlock the car, then opened the passenger door and waited for Tory to be installed inside.

She said, warm as ever, 'You must come again for dinner. Let me know how you get on at *Toi*.'

'Yes, thanks.' Tory smiled at the other woman whom she

had really liked—still did like—knowing she would never meet her again if she could help it.

'I'll explain to Luc,' Caro called out as they drew away from the kerb.

Tory managed a weak wave and felt a measure of relief once they were out of sight.

But Charlie drove only as far as the end of the crescent, before parking in the first available space and turning in his seat to stare at her, as if he still couldn't believe his eyes.

'I'm sorry.' Tory felt she owed him an apology. 'I had no idea. He never said.'

'*He?*'

'Lucas.'

'You came with him?' Charlie caught up with events. 'Oh, you're the production assistant from Eastwich.'

She gave a nod.

'My wife called you by some other name.' He frowned, trying to remember.

'Tory,' she supplied. 'It was my mother's name for me when I was little. I went back to using it after…'

She left it hanging. What to say otherwise? *After you dumped me?*

It was true enough. She'd reverted to Tory in a desire to reinvent the person she was, but he'd been more catalyst than cause. She looked at him now and felt not a single ounce of passion. How strange.

'And you didn't realise who Luc was?' Charlie concluded.

'No, I did,' she admitted. 'I realised when he took over Eastwich. It was just that he offered to introduce me to someone who'd worked on a woman's magazine—Eastwich is doing this documentary—and it wasn't until five minutes ago that the penny dropped who Caro actually was.'

'Right.' Charlie absorbed this information while still gazing at her intently. '*You* haven't changed. Not at all.'

Tory pulled a face, trying to lighten things up. 'I'm not sure that's good.'

Charlie remained serious. 'You're just the same, just the way I imagine you.'

Tory felt no satisfaction at the wistful note of regret in Charlie's voice. The past was dead for her.

'Your wife's lovely,' she said quite genuinely.

'Thanks,' he replied but it was as if she'd complimented him on a new car, and he added with more feeling, 'She's not you.'

Tory couldn't misunderstand his meaning, not when it went along with the soulful look in his eyes. It was the look he'd worn during their long-ago courtship, when she'd imagined herself in love with him, and he with her. But now, from a distance, she could see it had all been illusion.

'No, she's not,' she agreed at length. 'She's the woman who gave you the children you always wanted.'

It was a pointed remark that hit its target as he winced. 'That was cruel.'

'Was it?' Tory didn't care as she stated, 'It's a cruel world.'

'You've grown harder, Vicki.' He looked troubled by the idea.

Tory wondered what he expected. 'Life does that to people.'

'Yes… Yes, it does. You have no idea how much I wish—' She cut across him. 'Don't.'

'But you don't know what I'm going to say.' He reached for her hand.

She pulled it from his grasp. 'I don't want to know, Charlie. I think I'll get out here.'

'Please, Vicki,' he appealed, but she already had the door open and didn't stop even when he called out, 'You have to forgive me.'

She kept walking, wrapping her pashmina round her as the cool night air touched her bare shoulders. She didn't look back.

She didn't run. Charlie Wainwright didn't frighten her. In fact, he didn't do anything to her any more, except make her sorry for his wife.

It was a revelation. For years she had wondered if it was Charlie who had stopped her forming any other serious relationship. Always, at the back of her mind, had been the idea she might just still love him. And now? Nothing.

She couldn't even stay angry with him. As she walked the

Kensington streets, heading back towards the hotel, her anger switched to another man. A tall, blue-eyed, dark-haired American with a rather nasty sense of humour.

How else to explain what he'd done? It couldn't have been coincidence. It was too far a stretch.

So what had it been? A social experiment to check how she'd react when face to face with her former fiancé?

Well, tough luck, he'd missed it, playing favourite uncle to Charlie's kids.

It was Caro she felt sorry for. Married to a husband who, at best, was a wimp, and deceived by a man whom she imagined loyal enough to make him her sons' godfather.

No one could be a real friend and engineer such a situation. Even if the plan had been to stir up things for Tory, there had always been a danger of hurting Caro along the way. He must have known that. He was no fool.

But that was what really got to Tory. She'd spent almost the whole day with Lucas Ryecart, her barriers against him slipping away. It was only now she acknowledged that she'd dressed for him this evening. Only now she admitted how jealous she'd been, seeing him with that other woman at the bar. And, in watching him with his godsons, listening to Caro talking about him with such fondness, she had been seduced into seeing him in a different light.

She supposed she should be grateful for the wake-up call, otherwise she might have been in real danger of falling for the bastard. Now anger was uppermost and kept her buoyant until she finally reached her hotel.

She hadn't eaten since lunch and the walk had given her an appetite, but it had also given her sore feet—her shoes had been new and high-heeled—and she decided to order room service. An elaborate variety of courses was on offer and she considered running up a huge bill, courtesy of Eastwich and Lucas Ryecart, but she eventually settled for a salad, omelette and a chilled bottle of white wine to calm her down. She took her meal, watching a documentary on cheating husbands. It seemed an appropriate choice of viewing for that evening.

She was getting ready for bed, mellowed somewhat by the

wine, when there was a knock on the hotel room door. She assumed it was room service although they'd already cleared her dinner. She tied the hotel's fluffy bathrobe tighter round the waist and checked she was decent before opening the door.

One glance and, registering the figure standing on the threshold, she shut it immediately before Lucas could even think to get a foot in the door.

She ignored his next knock and the several after it, and the repetitions of her name, 'Tory!' and the appeals to, 'Open up,' and 'We have to talk.'

Tory didn't see they had to talk at all. In fact, she'd already decided a resignation letter would do for their next communication. She'd been mentally composing it all through supper and preparing for bed. But she had no desire to deliver it in person.

'*Tory*—' his tone changed to barely restrained anger '—I don't want to have to do this, but you're leaving me no choice.'

Do what? Tory scowled at the door. It was thick and made of real wood. Did he imagine he could run at it and break it down? She almost wished he'd try.

'Tory!' Her name was called once more, followed by a determined, 'Right.'

She waited in anticipation for his next move. She didn't really expect him to do anything as crude as batter on the door and she was right. She heard the click of the electronic locking system and then he was in the room before she had a chance to react.

He shut the door behind him, but didn't come further into the room as he drawled, 'Don't look so panic-stricken. I'm not going to jump on you.'

'How did you get that?' She indicated the card key in his hand.

'I told them I'd lost mine,' he relayed. 'They handed another over once I'd proved I was the registered occupant of the room.'

'How low can you get?' She didn't hide her contempt.

'Lower than that,' he rejoined without apology.

'Well…?' She waited for him to state his business.

He seemed in no hurry. 'You could offer me a drink,' he said as if he were an invited guest.

'I could call Security,' she countered with a hard edge.

'You could,' he agreed. 'Go ahead, if you want.'

He leaned against the door and folded his arms. It didn't seem to bother him.

'You're so sure I won't.' Tory tried to sound threatening.

He was unimpressed. 'Not sure, no, but I don't think you like scenes. Otherwise you might have hung around at the Wainwrights.'

'I'm sorry if you feel cheated.' Her tone was derisive.

His brows drew together. 'You think I'd have liked to watch the grand reunion?'

'Why else did you stage it?' she rallied.

'Hold on a minute.' He abandoned his relaxed pose. 'I had no idea you had any connection with the Wainwrights until I came downstairs to find you gone and an agitated Charlie in your place.'

Tory wasn't convinced. 'You expect me to believe that?'

'I've pretty much given up expecting anything of you,' he said, 'but, yes, I'm telling you straight—I was as much in the dark as you.'

'All right.' It rang true. On his part, anyway. She, of course, hadn't totally been in the dark.

She must have looked guilty as the blue eyes were already studying her, narrowed.

'Or maybe even more so?' he asked astutely.

Tory suddenly found herself on the defensive. 'I did not realise who we were visiting until about a minute before Charlie came home.'

A statement of fact; he still saw behind her carefully chosen words. 'But you knew of my connection to the Wainwrights. You must have.'

Tory considered denying it. After all, he'd never actually mentioned his wife by name or his in-laws. But what would be the point?

'I did realise, yes,' she admitted, 'the first day we met.'

'No wonder you seemed familiar.' His eyes hardened with distrust. 'I must have seen a photograph or something, though I guess you've changed in…what? Five years, would it be?'

She nodded. 'My hair was longer and I wore glasses before I had contacts fitted.'

'Why didn't you say anything?' he added.

'What, exactly?' countered Tory. ' I was once engaged to your late wife's brother? Not quite the easiest of introductions to a new boss.'

'You had plenty of chances later… Do you honestly think I would have taken you to their house, if I'd been clued up?' His tone clearly told her he wouldn't.

It seemed she'd misjudged him, yet again, but rather than apologise she gave an uninterested shrug.

It was a gesture designed to annoy, and annoy it did as his mouth went into a tight line and he finally stepped away from the door to cross the room.

Misunderstanding his purpose, Tory retreated to the far corner. She felt a little foolish when he veered off towards the mini-bar.

He noted her jumpiness with a humourless smile. 'Relax. Right at the moment a drink is all I want.'

If it was meant to reassure, it didn't. His eyes lingered long enough to suggest that later he might want something else.

Tory took a deep, steadying breath and told herself to keep calm. He was playing games, that was all.

'Can I fix you one?' He bent to do a quick inventory of, 'Whisky, gin, vodka, beer…'

'No…thank you.' Tory had already had several glasses of wine earlier.

She watched as he took a couple of miniature whiskies from the cabinet and poured both in a glass, then eased his length onto the only chair.

As hotel bedrooms went, it had seemed quite spacious, but, with him in it, it suddenly felt overcrowded.

'So what happened between you and Charlie?' he asked, as if his interest was merely casual.

'Tonight?'

'No, we'll come to that. I meant before.'

Tory supposed she could have told him to mind his own business, but wasn't that making it a big deal? And it wasn't. Not really. Not any more.

'We met at college on the same media course,' she relayed, 'we went out, then became briefly engaged before having second thoughts.'

'Which one of you?'

'Which one of you what?'

'Had second thoughts?'

Both of them, Tory supposed was the truth.

She'd had second thoughts from the moment Charlie had proposed and pressed her for an immediate answer at the New Year's party they'd been attending. But she'd tried hard to ignore her doubts and let herself be caught up in Charlie's impulsiveness and sheer certainty about everything.

'Charlie,' she answered at length.

'That's not what I heard,' he drawled back at her.

Tory wasn't altogether surprised. It was Charlie who'd decided to call off the engagement but she'd left it up to him as to what story he gave people.

'I heard,' he continued at her silence, 'that all of a sudden the engagement was off and Charlie was devastated. Doesn't quite tally with the notion he was the one to back out, now, does it?'

'Who did you hear it from?' she retorted. 'His mother?'

'As I recall, yes.' He nodded. 'Charlie wasn't making much sense at the time. He just said he'd discovered something that made it impossible for you to go on together.'

That was true enough and she supposed she was glad that Charlie had been discreet, although it was questionable whether his intention had been to save her face or his own.

'I bet his mother couldn't contain her delight.' Tory knew she'd never been good enough for Diana Wainwright.

He raised a brow at her slightly acerbic tone before admitting, 'She did think you were unsuited, yes.'

'Not her sort at all.' Tory mimicked the other woman's posh way of talking.

'Yeah, okay, Diana can be a bit of a snob,' he conceded, 'but she was more concerned for Charlie and whether he'd ever get over you.'

There was a note of accusation in his voice. It seemed he'd cast her in the role of heartbreaker.

Tory resented the unfairness of it. 'Well, she was wrong, wasn't she? How long before he was married? A year, maybe?'

'And you'd prefer him to do what?' he grated back. 'Stay crying into his beer? Carry a torch for ever? Or maybe go crawling back to you?'

'I didn't want that,' Tory denied angrily.

'No?' He clearly didn't believe her.

'No!' she repeated, gritting her teeth.

He still didn't look satisfied as he muttered, 'Let's hope not.'

'Does it matter?' Tory wasn't enjoying this trip down memory lane. 'It's past, over, history.'

'Is it?'

Why was he looking at her like that?

'Yes, of course,' she declared adamantly. ' I haven't seen Charlie for five years.'

'But you saw him tonight,' he reminded her, 'and he saw you.'

What was he getting at? Obviously something, but she'd lost the plot.

'Yes,' she answered slowly.

'And?' He waited.

She still didn't know what he wanted her to say.

'And nothing,' she replied.

'He gave you a ride, you shook hands like nice polite English people do and said goodbye?' The mocking drawl in his voice was shot through with disbelief.

Colour seeped into Tory's cheeks even as she told herself he couldn't possibly know otherwise. He'd not been in the car with them and surely Charlie hadn't rushed off home to confess all.

'Something along those lines,' she finally murmured.

It was the wrong answer, evidently, as his lips curled with

contempt for her. Then he drained his whisky and set the glass down on a table with a cracking noise, before rising to his feet.

She watched him cross to the door, seemingly with the intention of leaving.

She should have been relieved but instead she found herself coming round the end of the bed, pursuing him as she claimed, 'Nothing happened between us, if that's what you're trying to imply.'

He paused mid-flight, hand on the lock, back rigid, then turned round to face her.

'Nothing happened?' he echoed, but there was a dangerous edge to his voice, and when she took a step backwards he reached out to catch her arm.

Unable to retreat, Tory stood shaking her head. 'I—I... No, nothing.'

'Liar.' The word was growled at her as he drew her closer. 'I just sat through dinner with a man who looked like a ghost had come back to haunt him. I spent most of it trying to distract his wife so she wouldn't notice how sappy he was acting, then afterwards had to listen while Charlie went on like a corny Country and Western song about the love of his life and how he'd lost her.'

And he blamed it all on her. Tory saw that in the scathing look he gave her.

'I'm not interested in Charlie,' she said in her own defence.

'And that makes it better?' It was a rhetorical question as he ran on, 'So why vamp him—to see if you could? Or a little revenge?'

'*Vamp him?*' Tory repeated, her own temper rising. 'Is that what Charlie said?'

'He didn't need to,' Lucas replied. 'It was obvious from the way he was behaving. Doesn't it mean anything to you, the fact he's married, has kids?'

She shook her head, denying that she'd done anything, but he chose to misunderstand, to believe the worst of her.

'Evidently not,' he concluded for himself. 'Well, I'm warning you now, go near Charlie again and I'll make sure you regret it.'

'Really?' The threat didn't scare Tory, it just made her madder. 'So how are you going to do that, Mr Ryecart? Let me guess? My P45 in the post.'

'P45?' The term didn't translate.

'P45, it's a tax form you get when you stop working for a company—' Tory switched to saying, 'Never mind. It doesn't matter. You can't sack me because I quit. As of now, this moment.'

It clearly took him by surprise as his brows arched together. Perhaps he'd imagined he was the only one who could call the shots.

'You can't quit!' he barked back.

'Oh, can't I?' Tory taunted, and tried to jerk her hands free.

He held them fast, long fingers circling her slender wrists. 'You're on contract and in the middle of an assignment. I thought you were the one who could keep work and their personal life separate?'

Tory recognised the claim she'd made that afternoon but didn't appreciate having it flung back at her.

'And this business with you and Charlie,' he continued heavily, 'has absolutely nothing to do with work, and everything to do with Caro and those three kids back there. You honestly want to wreck their lives just because Charlie was too spineless to marry you in the first place?'

Of course Tory didn't. No thought could be further from her mind, but his lecturing tone incensed her all the same.

'Why not?' she found herself saying. 'You don't expect anything better of me, do you? You imagine I'll sleep with anyone, after all... Well, anyone but you, that is,' she added with reckless intent.

She didn't regret it. Not then, anyway. She enjoyed wiping that superior look from his face.

It was replaced with a cloud of dark anger. 'You think I'd want to sleep with you now?'

His tone said he'd not touch her, but his eyes said something else, and Tory scoffed at him, 'Yes, actually, I do.'

She felt his hands tighten like bands round her arms, and waited for him to push her away.

But she had seriously miscalculated.

'Let's see, shall we?' he ground back, pulling her towards him.

At the last moment she tried to turn but it was too late. His hand was in her hair, holding her head steady. She saw his mouth curve into a humourless smile a second before it lowered on hers.

She meant to resist but she had forgotten how it felt to be kissed by this man. His lips moved against hers, warm and hard and persuasive, tongue tasting teeth until she opened to him, then thrusting inside to explore the warm, sweet intimacy of her mouth, making her breathing as ragged as his.

'You're right,' he murmured against her mouth. 'I still want you.'

It was the last they spoke, the last conscious thought formed as desire overwhelmed reason.

Afterwards Tory would try to tell herself it was down to the drink they'd both had. Afterwards she'd try to call it seduction but then she'd remember how it really had been. Too quick to be seduction. Too sweet to be force.

It was more compulsion as he began to touch her, a hand moving round, slipping inside her robe, pushing aside, seeking flesh, breasts swollen and heavy, fingering until she cried out for the mouth closing, sucking on her aching nipples. It was need and desperation as she fell with him on the bed and guided him down to the part of her that was already warm and wet and let him stroke her, deep and intimate, until desire kicked in her belly and she drew his hips to hers.

She was naked, he still clothed. Together they fumbled for his zip. Then they coupled in mutual need.

The first thrust and he filled her too completely. She moaned a little until his mouth covered hers in a sweet, drugging kiss. Then slowly he moved inside her and her body opened up as if it had always known his, and she rose and fell with him, grasping his shoulders, digging in at each shaft, panting and gasping, almost one being as they came together with wild, unrestrained pleasure.

They lay back on the bed, for a while suspended in time,

their bodies experiencing intense physical satisfaction—then gradually reality impinged and the mind took back control.

Tory remained paralysed in those first conscious moments, wondering what she had done. She'd never made love like that, with almost primitive urgency. She'd never felt like this, possessed to the core. She'd never wanted to let a man this close to her.

Every instinct told her to run. She'd nowhere to go but inside her head. So she retreated there as she slid off the bed and picked up the robe she'd been wearing and turned her back to him as she put it on.

Somehow Luc wasn't surprised by this reaction. He was more surprised by what had gone before.

He followed her up off the bed, straightening his clothes as he did so. He considered an apology but it would have been hypocrisy. He wasn't sorry for what he'd done. In fact, when he recalled her response, so warm and passionate, he wanted to do it all over again.

Her rigid stance, however, told him the cold war had resumed.

He restrained a desire to cross the room and take her back in his arms.

'You want me to go?' he surmised instead.

'Yes.' Tory didn't risk saying more.

He was equally laconic. 'Okay.'

But still Tory didn't imagine he would leave without another word, didn't believe it when she heard the door behind her open and shut.

She turned and found herself in an empty room. He was gone. Just like that.

But he couldn't be forgotten the same way. How could he be when he'd left his mark on her body, left a jagged tear on her heart?

She showered and tried to wash the smell of him, the taste of him, the touch of him from her body. She leaned against cool white tiles while hot tears of shame and rejection ran down her cheeks. She towelled her skin dry till it hurt and climbed into the crumpled bed and shut her eyes tight and prayed for sleep to come.

But it made no difference. When finally she slipped away, she found him chasing through her dreams.

It seemed as if she had opened a door that she couldn't close.

CHAPTER EIGHT

TORY woke, hoping it really had been a dream, but her eyes were drawn to the whisky glass on the table. This trace of Lucas's presence prompted vivid recall of what had happened last night.

She felt a measure of shame. She'd never indulged before in casual sex but what Lucas and she had done together could scarcely be described as anything else. And the worst part was the way he'd left her, as if he hadn't been able to wait to be gone.

She wondered how she could ever face him again. The easy option was not to. She could follow through her threat to quit her job. In the cool light of day, however, she knew such an action would damage her career as well as her finances.

And what else had she but work? It was the thing she did best, the thing that gave her life meaning and form. If she walked away from Eastwich now, how long might it be before she secured another post?

There was also a reasonable possibility that Lucas would no longer be a problem. Yes, he'd pursued her from the moment they'd met, but now he'd had her and used her and seemingly lost interest at once. Perhaps she was already history.

Tory visualised their next meeting. She'd be churned up inside while he would be his usual laid-back self. He might or might not allude to their one-night stand. If he did, it would be as a joke or a shrugged aside. No big deal. Couldn't she act the same way, regardless of how she felt inside?

Tory decided she could and would, and, driven by a mixture of pride and pragmatism, she got herself out of bed, showered and dressed and ready for her first day as an employee of *Toi*.

While she'd been nervous yesterday, she approached today very differently. She sailed into the offices with an almost reckless disregard as to whether she was found out or not, and straight away set up a meeting with her three assistants, listening as they explained the work in progress before making appropriate comments and suggesting approaches that might be taken for this or that article. She made it clear that they would have a fair degree of autonomy, and two of the young women seemed happy to accept her as their new boss. The third was Sam Hollier who'd been Acting Features Editor, and, not surprisingly, she was more hostile, although she stopped short of outright rebellion, and Tory decided she could probably handle her.

It was Amanda Villiers of whom she was most wary, but, to her relief, the lady in question failed to appear. Either she was too busy to bother or didn't really care whether Tory settled to the job or not.

Thus Tory survived the day with her credibility intact and actually stayed late, wading through some unsolicited articles sent by freelance writers. Most she earmarked for polite rejections, a couple were worth considering and one stood out as eminently printable. Unsure if she had the authority to commission the latter, she decided to play safe and placed a copy on Amanda's desk, requesting her opinion of it.

She returned to the hotel with some reluctance. Occupied throughout the day, she'd avoided thinking of Lucas Ryecart, but once back in her room she was unable to keep her mind off the events of last night. She felt she would have welcomed any distraction until Reception rang up to her room, informing her she had a visitor downstairs: Caro Wainwright.

Tory assumed it was a social call—perhaps Caro offering further work advice. Much as she'd liked her, Tory felt pursuing even the most tenuous relationship with her was inadvisable. But refusing to see her at all might prompt some suspicions in Caro's mind.

Tory resolved to go down and do her best to act normally. She greeted Caro with a polite smile and hid her surprise at the other woman's attire—an orange and black track suit over a running top.

'It's one of my gym nights,' explained Caro, 'but I decided at the last moment to come here…see how you were.'

'Much better,' Tory volunteered.

'That's good,' Caro murmured back.

Silence followed these pleasantries until Tory felt almost obliged to add, 'We could go for a drink in the lounge bar.'

Caro nodded even as she looked uncertain. 'Perhaps there's a dress code.'

Tory glanced towards a group of young men exiting the bar in question. They wore an array of scruffy denim jackets and tie-less shirts flapping loosely over jeans.

'Not from the look of that lot, there isn't,' she remarked on their dress.

Caro followed her gaze. 'Aren't they some pop group or other?'

'Possibly,' agreed Tory, before leading the way through the glass doors.

They gravitated towards a booth at the back. Tory insisted on buying the drinks and escaped to the bar. It gave her some precious minutes to compose herself.

When she returned, Caro took a good swig of the gin and tonic she'd requested.

It was Dutch courage, as she resumed, 'I'm not really sure what I want to say. I got myself riled up to come here but didn't think much further than that.'

Tory felt her stomach drop. It didn't take a genius to conclude from Caro's words, 'You know who I am, don't you?'

Caro nodded slowly.

'Lucas told you?' added Tory, a note of accusation creeping into her voice.

'When I asked him, he did,' relayed Caro, 'but not last night.'

Tory frowned, trying to sort out exactly what this meant.

Caro ran on, 'I knew there was something wrong at dinner. Charlie was acting really oddly but I thought it had something to do with work. Then, while I was making coffee, Luc changed his mind about staying and Charlie got very agitated at the idea that Luc had gone off to spend the night with you.'

'He didn't.' Tory could deny that at least.

'No, I know,' Caro stated. 'Luc told me he stayed with Chuck, his stepfather.'

So that was where he'd gone. Tory imagined the two men together, discussing Luc's latest acquisition—her! She just hoped she was being unduly paranoid.

'Anyway, Charlie thought otherwise,' Caro continued. 'In fact, to be honest, so did I. I made some joke about it—something about Luc meeting his match—and Charlie went ballistic. He made out he was upset because of his sister's memory, although he usually admired Luc for his success with women. It took me a while to figure out he minded for himself, not his sister…' Caro tailed off and her face reflected the pain she felt.

Tory wanted to say something. She just wasn't sure what. She was scared of making the situation worse.

Eventually she murmured, 'Charlie told you who I was.'

Caro shook her head. 'I guessed later, lying in bed, waiting for him to come up. I remembered your reaction to Charlie's name—your sudden bout of illness. It was obvious then that you knew him. I was just too stupid to realise it.'

'It's me that was stupid—' Tory sighed in response '—not realising who you were. I would never have gone to your house if I had.'

Caro's eyes rested on her, testing her sincerity, before she said, 'Well, it's too late to change things. The question is where we go from here.'

'I'm not sure I understand,' Tory replied carefully.

'Look, I know Charlie's rung you,' Caro informed her. 'I overheard him this morning, asking to speak to Victoria Lloyd. That's you, isn't it?'

Tory looked genuinely blank. 'I never received any calls.'

'He must have missed you,' Caro concluded, 'but that hardly matters. The fact that he's calling you at all is the issue.'

Tory could see that and ventured a possibility. 'Maybe he was calling to apologise. He *was* somewhat rude to me last night.'

'Rude?' Caro echoed in surprise.

'I'd say so. Claimed I'd grown very hard, ' Tory could relay quite truthfully, 'which is a bit of a cheek, coming from him. I mean, you know he dumped me, don't you?'

'Well, I...' Caro looked confused. 'I was never quite sure what had happened between you.'

'Not ready to commit.' Tory pulled a face. 'That's what he said. Rubbish, of course. I mean, he was ready enough when he met you a few months later, wasn't he?'

'I...um...yes, I suppose,' Caro agreed in apologetic tones.

'Well, you're welcome to him.' Tory gave a negligent shrug before reaching for her drink.

Over the rim she watched Caro's changing expressions. Having come here to warn Tory off or perhaps plead with her, Caro had not anticipated this outcome. She looked as if she couldn't quite believe things were going to be so easily resolved.

'God, jealousy does make fools of people. I really thought that you and him...' She trailed off and gave her a sheepish look. 'I wish now I'd listened to Luc.'

'Luc?' Tory repeated more sharply. 'What did he say?'

'I...' Caro hesitated, not wanting to commit another *faux pas*. 'Just that he didn't think you'd be interested in Charlie, that you had someone else.'

'When did he say this?'

'This morning when I phoned him on his mobile and started blubbering my suspicions.'

Tory's eyes darkened. She was beginning to form some suspicions of her own. What Luc and she had done last night, she'd put down to sexual urges and momentary impulses. She hadn't considered it a premeditated act on his part.

But what if it was? What if he'd slept with her entirely to discredit her in Charlie's eyes?

'He offered to tell Charlie as much—' Caro seemed to confirm the idea '—although he was convinced that I had the wrong end of the stick, which, of course, it appears I had... I really do feel a Class A Idiot.'

'That makes two of us.' Tory spoke her thoughts aloud.

'Two?' Caro raised a brow.

But Tory shook her head. Caro was never going to believe what a rat Lucas Ryecart had been to her.

'I've been making an idiot of myself all day,' Tory confided instead.

Caro was suitably distracted. 'The magazine, of course! How did it go?'

'You do not want to know.' Tory rolled her eyes, conveying disaster, and the two exchanged smiles.

It was a spontaneous reaction but the smiles soon faded. In other circumstances they could have been friends, but neither wished to risk it, Caro because her husband's ex-fiancée was prettier, smarter and a whole lot nicer than anyone in the family had led her to believe, and Tory, because Caro was too much like family to Lucas Ryecart.

So they finished their drinks, shook hands and parted company in the lobby.

Tory then went to the desk and, asking if there were any messages, collected several slips of paper.

There were four, three from Charlie, the last asking her to call him on his mobile. The message would have been easy to ignore but seemed safer to answer, and sooner rather than later.

Back in her bedroom, she dialled the mobile number given, and, when Charlie said his name, didn't give him much chance to say anything else. Spurred on by the sounds of children playing in the background, she told him straight. She didn't know why he'd been calling her, didn't want to know why unless it was to apologise for last night's rudeness, didn't want him to call again. If he did keep calling, then she would have to inform her rugby-playing boyfriend who would happily reconvey her message in person.

Charlie just managed to bluster out the words, 'Are you threatening me?' before Tory replied with a resounding, 'Yes,' and replaced the receiver with a decisive click.

Till that point she hadn't known she had such a ruthless streak. She rather liked it. In fact, it had felt positively liberating to say exactly what one thought.

She looked at the other message in her hand. She'd read it before her call to Charlie. It was brief enough:

'CALL ME. IT'S IMPORTANT. LUCAS.'

In fact, it couldn't be briefer. No one would have known they were lovers. Correction, *had* been lovers. Once. And that was one time too many.

Tory reached for the phone again and dialled an outside line, but that was as far as she got. Having vented her spleen on Charlie, she'd wasted precious reserves of anger and Lucas was nowhere near as easy to handle.

She returned the mouthpiece to its cradle. Silence was surely the best show of contempt. She limited herself to tearing the message into a hundred tiny pieces.

Tory realised, of course, that she couldn't avoid Luc for ever, not if he wanted to talk to her, but she gave it her best shot.

When her mobile rang the next day, displaying a number she didn't know, she switched it off rather than answer it, and when Lucas called the magazine's number directly, she was 'in conference' in the morning and 'out of the building' in the afternoon, lies happily relayed by the switchboard operator, Liz. The said Liz was a self-professed hater of men—having been recently dumped by one herself—and didn't need much persuasion to come up with varied excuses why Tory was perpetually unavailable.

Tory did, however, take a call from Alex.

He was ostensibly phoning to find out how she was doing, but, after some pretty token interest, launched into his own news. It seemed that Rita, his wife, had finally agreed to his coming up to Scotland to visit the children. Alex hoped to go that weekend, depending on whether he found a flat in the interim.

Tory saw where he was going and didn't wait for him to get there. Yes, he could stay another week. But only on condition that he did go to Scotland.

Alex assured her he would. In fact, he confided his intention to try and win back his wife's affections. Tory made encouraging noises although personally she felt he had more chance of winning the London marathon on crutches.

Then, almost as an afterthought, he said, 'By the way, you

have to phone Ryecart. There's been some new developments you should know about. I offered to pass on a message but he doesn't seem to trust me.'

'Snap.' He didn't trust Tory either.

Alex laughed briefly before advising, 'I'd do it soon,' and signing off with a, 'Good luck for the weekend.'

Tory was left wondering about the nature of these so-called new developments. Was it on the work front or the Wainwright business? If she could be sure it was the latter, then she'd ignore the royal command. But what if it were work—what if she were about to be exposed at *Toi* for the impostor she undoubtedly was?

She was still deliberating the matter at the end of the day and left the offices without calling him. She didn't feel ready to talk to Lucas, whatever the reason. She went back to the hotel for another night and ordered room service.

She'd just finished her meal when the reception desk put through a call from an Alex Simpson.

'Alex, what now?' she asked with an impatient edge to her voice.

'Is that the way you normally talk to your boss?' a voice drawled back.

'You!' She almost spat the word down the line.

'Yes, me,' Lucas agreed and pre-empted her next move with, 'Don't hang up! Otherwise I'll keep calling all night.'

'I could ask Reception to block your calls,' she countered.

'My calls—or Alex's?' he threw back.

'I…' Tory asked herself why she was even having this conversation. 'Calls from anyone with an American accent,' she added at length.

'I can do British,' he replied and proceeded to prove the point with, 'I say, old bean, could I speak to Miss Lloyd, room two three five?'

'They'll know you're a fraud,' she retaliated. 'No one says "old bean" these days.'

'Old chap?' he supplanted.

Tory breathed heavily in response and, resigned, asked, 'What do you want?'

'Well, why don't we start with an apology?'

'An apology!'

'From me to you.'

'Oh.'

Tory waited.

'I shouldn't have sounded off about you and Charlie the other night.'

Tory waited another moment before saying, 'Is that it?'

'Pretty much,' he confirmed.

Tory's silence conveyed the fact that she was unimpressed.

'Unless you want it written in blood,' he suggested in a far from repentant tone.

'That would be a start,' she muttered back.

'Look,' he conceded, 'I'd apologise for the rest, only it would be hypocrisy. I'm *not* sorry we made love. In fact, I'd like to do it again, maybe a bit slower next time.'

Tory was glad he was at the other end of a phone line, although she should be used to his directness by now. His casual attitude to sex was no surprise, either, but it hurt all the same.

'And take pictures for Charlie, perhaps?' she finally ground back.

'What?'

'That's the idea, isn't it? To discredit me?'

'What?' he echoed with total incredulity. 'You think I slept with you so I could boast of the fact to Charlie?'

Did she think that? Tory wasn't sure any more. But she wasn't about to backtrack.

'I haven't said one word to Charlie,' he resumed through gritted teeth. 'It isn't me he's been calling.'

Tory didn't have to go looking for the accusing note in his voice.

'That's hardly my fault,' she retorted, 'and, for your information, I have told Charlie exactly how things stand. Check if you don't believe me. I have also reassured Caro that I have no designs on her husband.'

'You called Caro?'

'Correction, she called on me. Here at the hotel.'

'I told her not to do that.' He sighed heavily. 'What did you say to her?'

'Why don't you ask her?' suggested Tory.

'I will,' he countered.

He clearly didn't trust her. He still saw her as home-wrecker material. Forget the fact she was good enough for *him* to sleep with. Or perhaps bad enough was nearer the mark?

'So, if that's all—' Tory assumed they had no more to say to each other.

'I have a full diary the rest of the week,' he continued regardless, 'but we should meet up on Friday.'

'You and Caro?'

'No, you and I.'

Tory considered the prospect, before reminding them both, 'I'm off to the Derbyshire Dales doing outdoor activities.'

'I know,' he claimed.

It left Tory a little mystified. If he knew, then why...?

'How's it going at *Toi*, by the way?' he added, distracting her.

She'd thought he'd never ask. 'Easier than expected and more interesting.'

'Not considering defection, are we?'

'I wasn't, but now you mention it...'

He laughed. 'Are you sure—all those bitchy women?'

'You imagine they're any worse than Simon and Alex?' she countered without thinking.

The trouble was she kept forgetting Lucas Ryecart had two personae—careless, skirt-chasing ex-journalist and serious media boss who happened to own Eastwich.

'I didn't mean that,' she added quickly.

'Yes, you did,' he drawled back, 'but I'll forget you said it. I'll form my own opinion of those two in time, anyway.'

Tory assumed he already had.

'Meanwhile,' he continued, 'I thought you should know that I won't be broadcasting what happened between us the other night, in case that's of concern to you.'

It was, of course. Tory didn't want a reputation for sleeping with her boss, a reputation which might follow her round the industry.

'Thank you,' she said simply.

'Our business,' he replied with a quiet sincerity.

It was another trait of the man. As direct as he could be, he was also discreet.

'Quite,' she murmured back.

Both fell silent for a moment, aware of a rare accord. Tory half expected him to follow it up with another request for a date. She was debating her answer when he spoke again.

'In fact, next time we meet,' he suggested, 'let's pretend we don't know each other.'

'I...' Taken aback, Tory took moments to recover before she bristled with offence. 'Good idea!'

'Believe me, it will be,' he replied, tone cryptic.

It was as if he were up to something. But what?

Tory didn't get the chance to probe further as he signed off with the words, 'I'll be thinking about you till then.'

Tory was left holding a dead line. She stared at it, confused by the mixed messages he was sending. He wanted to forget about her *and* think about her. It didn't make sense.

Or maybe it did. She, too, wanted to forget what had happened between them. She didn't want to lie in bed, night after night, reliving his kiss, his touch, their coming together. But she did.

It was like having a film running continuously in her head. Each time she saw it, remarkably it seemed more real, more beautiful. Each time it left her shot with physical longing.

She felt like a voyeur, not recognising herself in the girl who twined her body with Lucas's and licked the sweat of his skin and spread her legs wide and drew him into her and moaned in pleasure as he penetrated her.

She wanted to destroy the film yet she kept viewing it. She tried to edit it, to have the girl reluctant, to make the man weak, inept, but she couldn't sublimate the truth, couldn't wipe out the image of Lucas as lover, strong and powerful, encountering no resistance as she accommodated his flesh and moved for him and rose to him and welcomed each thrust of pleasure until he finally took her, groaning her name as he staked his claim.

No one had ever possessed her like that. And somehow she knew no one else ever would. She didn't call it love. She *wouldn't* call it love. But whatever it was, it still frightened her witless.

Forget they'd ever met? If only she could.

CHAPTER NINE

'HE MUST be joking!' cried Amanda Villiers as they drew up beside a dirt track where the group from *Vitalis* was already waiting.

The co-ordinator from the outdoor activity centre had just announced that they were to walk the rest of the way, carrying their luggage.

Tory wasn't the only one hiding a smile as Amanda's designer suitcases were unloaded from the boot. They had been told to travel light—no more than a rucksack of essentials—but Amanda had chosen to disregard this instruction.

'How far is it?' someone asked.

'Not far.' The driver smiled briefly. 'Two miles, maybe.'

'Two miles!' shrieked Amanda with unfeigned horror. 'I can't carry these two miles.'

'No,' the co-ordinator agreed, but didn't offer any other comment.

Instead he began to explain that they were to proceed in pairs with an assigned member of the other group, leaving at three-minute intervals.

So Amanda directed at Tory, 'You'll have to take one of these.'

If she'd begged or even asked politely, Tory might have given it some consideration, but Amanda had been particularly bloody to her over the last two days and, now they'd left the offices of *Toi* behind, she no longer felt any need to go along with her.

'No, I won't,' she answered simply. 'You shouldn't have packed so much.'

'What?' Amanda obviously couldn't believe her ears.

'Didn't you read the booklet?' Tory ran on, positively enjoying her rebellion.

Amanda visibly fumed but to no avail. Tory's name was called out and she departed without a backward glance, accompanied by her 'twin' from the other team.

He introduced himself as Richard Lake, the features editor for *Vitalis*. It was the same role Tory was pretending to fill for *Toi*, and as they fell in step he wasted no time in quizzing her on her experience. When she revealed she'd worked at *Toi* just one short week, he initially looked cheered by the fact, then more pensive.

'Someone must rate you,' was his eventual comment. 'At *Vitalis* we've been told to limp on with the staff we have until M day.'

'M day?'

'Merger day.'

'You've been told, then,' Tory said somewhat foolishly.

It drew a sharp glance. 'Not for definite, no, but you obviously have.'

'I...' Tory tried to backtrack. 'Not really. Just speculation, that's all.'

He looked unconvinced and, with a resentful tightening of the lips, forged ahead of her.

Tory sensed the weekend was going to be somewhat tense if everyone shared the same paranoia. She supposed it would make for a better documentary although she was already having ethical reservations about spying on these people.

Not that it was being done surreptitiously. In the literature on the weekend, it had stated in the small print that much of the trip would be videoed and, when they'd disembarked from the minibus, there had been one of the centre workers, dressed in one of their distinctive green uniforms, wielding a camera in the background.

Tory was willing to guess it had been trained on a querulous Amanda but it was debatable whether Amanda had noticed it. Surely she wouldn't have behaved so pettishly if she had?

Tory wondered how Amanda was surviving the walk. It wasn't particularly rough terrain but, to someone unused to exercise, it could prove arduous.

Richard, Tory's own companion, had started off at a cracking pace but, after the first mile, showed definite signs of flagging. Tory, on the other hand, was more prepared through weekly aerobics classes, squash-playing and windsurfing.

'Let's stop for a moment,' Richard suggested as they came to a wooden stile.

'Why not?' Tory wasn't tired but she could see he was suffering. 'New boots?'

He glanced up from loosening his laces and decided she was being sympathetic rather than gloating as he admitted, 'Brand spanking new. Had to buy them because I had nothing else... Do you go walking?'

He regarded her scuffed boots with some envy.

'I spent a holiday, two summers ago, tramping round the Lake District with a friend.'

'Strictly a city man myself.' He made to take one boot off.

'I wouldn't unless you have plasters,' advised Tory. 'You may struggle to get it back on.'

'I suppose you're right,' he conceded. 'Best get going. Perhaps you'd set the pace.'

'Sure.' Tory climbed over the stile and started trudging up the next field, keeping a wary eye on some rather loudly mooing cattle.

She was relieved for a limping Richard when they reached the centre. A collection of old stone buildings, it was positioned on top of a hill. In its driveway were the two minibuses which had brought the groups from London.

There was a reception committee of uniformed staff waiting for them at the entrance. Tory didn't expect to recognise anyone and just stopped her jaw from dropping when she did.

Fortunately she was too shocked to speak and possibly betray them both.

Lucas Ryecart was totally composed, of course, but then *he* obviously expected to see *her*.

'I'm Luc.' He introduced himself in the same fashion as the others had. 'I'll be acting as an observer this weekend.'

'Pleased to meet you,' Richard murmured in polite return.

Tory didn't manage any greeting but her heart was beating so loudly she imagined the whole world could hear it. As well as shock, she'd felt a rush of pleasure at seeing him again. It seemed she wasn't cured at all.

A smile played on Lucas's mouth as he added, 'We'll speak later.'

He directed the comment to both of them, but his eyes dwelled on Tory, passing a silent message on.

Then a woman from the centre claimed their attention, leading them to their sleeping quarters. Tory followed on automatic pilot, nodding at the whereabouts of washing facilities and dining areas as they passed by on their way to the dormitories.

Assigned a bottom bunk in a room for six, Tory slumped down on it the moment the woman departed with Richard. She made no move to unpack her gear but sat hugging her knees and trying to come to terms with Lucas's sudden materialisation.

All week she'd worked hard to get him out of her head while every night he'd chased through her dreams and fantasies. Now here he was, large as life and irrepressible as ever.

It made sense now, of course, that last telephone conversation they'd shared. They were to pretend they didn't know each other next time they met. Next time being this time. He'd been preparing her.

But why? Why not tell her straight he'd be here, masquerading as one of the staff? Weren't they meant to be on the same side, working for the same aim?

The answer seemed obvious and any pleasure at seeing him again went sour. He didn't trust her. Not even on a professional level. He'd given her his pet project and then had second thoughts about her capabilities. She felt both hurt and angry.

Her face must have reflected this as another arrival was shown into the dormitory and asked, 'Are you all right?'

'Yes, fine,' Tory lied and began finally to unpack her rucksack.

'I'm not,' the woman continued. 'Bloody forced march! I'm Mel, by the way.'

'Tory,' offered Tory.

Mel looked disconcerted. 'Not especially. Why do you want to know?'

It took Tory a moment to realise they were talking at cross purposes. 'No, sorry, you've misunderstood. My name's Tory—short for Victoria.'

'Oh, right.' The other girl laughed at her mistake. 'I thought for a mad moment you were a recruiter for the Conservative Party. Can't abide politics, myself. Or politicians. Greasy bunch, the lot of them.'

Tory thought that a rather sweeping statement but smiled all the same.

'I take it you're with *Toi*,' enquired Mel.

'Yes, Features Editor.' Tory had said this so often she almost believed it herself.

'I'm Advertising Sales for *Vitalis*,' relayed Mel, 'or I was when we left the office.'

'You've been promoted?' Tory queried.

'I wish.' Mel pulled a face. 'No, I just reckon no one can count on being who they were before this weekend.'

'You think it's some kind of test.'

'What else?'

'A bonding exercise prior to *Toi* and *Vitalis* merging.'

The suggestion drew a sceptical look from Mel. 'You believe that?'

Tory shrugged rather than express another opinion. She wasn't there to stir things up.

'No, it's survival of the fittest,' ran on Mel, 'or maybe the sanest after a whole weekend of closed confinement. Still, there might be some compensations. Some pretty *fit* instructors, did you notice?'

'Not really.' Tory had been too busy noticing Lucas.

'Don't tell me—you're engaged, married or blind?' Mel bantered back.

Tory shook her head, joking back, 'Single but choosy.'

'*Very*,' agreed Mel, 'if Mr America didn't do anything for you.'

Tory might have known it. Of all the men at the centre over whom Mel could have drooled, it had to be Lucas that had caught her eye.

'You must have seen him,' she ran on. 'Dark hair. Sexy

mouth. Come-to-bed eyes. And when he spoke, oh, God, I swear I fell in love right then and there!'

Mel was exaggerating, of course. At least Tory assumed she was. But it didn't help Tory, knowing other women were just as susceptible to him.

'Yes, the weekend is definitely looking up,' Mel observed with a wicked smile.

Tory felt a great pang of jealousy. She looked at Mel, tall, blonde and more than passingly pretty, and wondered if she were his type. Probably.

Probably they all were. Every woman silly enough to fall for amused blue eyes and a handsome face.

'You're welcome to him!' she told Mel and nearly believed it herself.

'Girl, you don't know what you're missing. Still, I'm not complaining. The less competition, the better. What are the rest of your team like?'

Tory wasn't sure what Mel was asking—for a rundown of their personalities or their appearance. 'I don't know them that well. I only joined the magazine this week.'

'I see.' Mel gave her an appraising look. 'No point in asking pointers on how you put up with your cow of an editor-in-chief, then?'

'Not really, no.' Tory had no inclination to defend Amanda.

'Because I've heard she's the front runner to be El Supremo,' confided Mel, 'of the new hag mag.'

Hag mag? That was a new one on Tory as she speculated on how Amanda would cope with Mel's outspokenness. Not a relationship that promised much mileage, she thought.

'You could try laughing at her jokes,' suggested Tory, 'while practising the words, "Yes, Amanda, no, Amanda, three bags full, Amanda".'

'God, that bad?' Mel rolled her eyes. 'How do you put up with it.'

Tory shrugged, suggesting indifference. She could hardly explain how temporary her role in *Toi* was.

Mel continued to gaze at her curiously and Tory worried a little if here was someone smart enough to blow her cover.

Further conversation, however, was curtailed by the arrival of more course members. They came limping in at intervals, and talk revolved around sore feet, uncomfortable beds and pointless exercises. Tory hoped the bunk left unoccupied longest was for someone other than Amanda, but that hope was dashed when she eventually made an entrance, complaining bitterly at the ruination of her new designer boots and jeans. She made no mention of the scruffy old backpack she was carrying but it wasn't hard to work out that it was on loan from the centre, a condensed replacement for all the suitcases she'd packed.

Fortunately she moaned to Sam Hollier, Tory's erstwhile assistant, and contented herself with shooting Tory venomous looks until the dinner bell was rung.

The meal of pasta and salad was well cooked and put people in better spirits. It was still very much a case of them and us, however, with the staff from *Toi* seated round one bench table and *Vitalis* grouped round another.

At the end of the room sat the centre staff in their distinctive green sweatshirts. Tory risked a quick glance in their direction and saw Lucas engaged in conversation with an athletic-looking girl in her mid-twenties. Tory's mouth thinned. Trust him to home in on the prettiest member of staff.

She tore her eyes away and dragged her mind back to the task in hand. She wasn't here to monitor Lucas Ryecart's charm rating but to concentrate on the documentary-making potential of their situation.

There was certainly a general air of dissension about the weekend, some already refusing to go caving or climbing if either activity was suggested. All considered the course to be pointless.

Tory had doubts, too. She could see the theory behind it. If the magazines did merge, the staff from each would have to be integrated so meeting on neutral ground might help reduce suspicion and rivalry. Currently, however, it was serving to increase paranoia.

After the meal, they were all shepherded into a communal room for what Tom Mackintosh, the head of the centre, described as fun and games. Reactions were mixed. Participants either looked tense, regarding it as the start of 'testing', or feigned indifference.

For their first task, they were forbidden to talk before being given a piece of paper with a number, from one to twelve, on it, and blindfolded. They then had to arrange themselves in a line in ascending order from the platform to the back of the hall.

It sounded simple but wasn't. The only way of conveying a number was to tap it out on people's hands and, though one could quickly find a neighbouring number, it was some time before they devised a method of stamping feet to establish a way of ordering the line. By that time the fun element had kicked in and there was much stifled laughter as they tried to adhere to the silence rule while grasping hands and swapping about and half tripping over each other.

It took longer than they would have imagined but there was a definite sense of triumph when they finally established with hand-squeezing codes that they were in line.

It certainly broke the ice and they followed this exercise by giving, in turn, a brief account of themselves.

The majority talked of themselves in terms of work but a few concentrated on their life outside. Tory decided to avoid spinning any tales she couldn't support and gave out true personal details like her age, single status and interests.

Afterwards they were divided into three groups of four and sent to corners of the room to tackle their next assignment, involving a sedentary treasure hunt of cryptic clues and intricate Ordnance Survey maps. It demanded lateral thinking as well as map-reading, but the real object was to get them to co-operate as a team in order to solve the mystery first. As an added incentive, the prize was a chilled bottle of champagne in an otherwise alcohol-free zone.

Tory was in the same group as Richard, her opposite number on *Vitalis*. He'd mellowed since their earlier walk together and she discovered he was both smart and witty. She was smiling at his jokes even before she became aware of Lucas observing them from a discreet distance. After that she smiled that little bit harder while stopping just short of giving Richard any wrong ideas. Their table didn't win but came a close second and gave each other consolation hugs.

Tory was tidying maps, guard down, when Lucas finally approached. 'I'll show you where they go.'

Tory could hardly refuse the offer and fell in step with him as they walked to a store cupboard at the far end.

'Are you trying to make me jealous, by any chance?' he murmured when they were out of earshot.

Guilty as charged, Tory nevertheless snapped, 'Of course not!'

'Well, you're managing it anyway,' he drawled back.

Tory risked a glance in his direction. He didn't look in the least bit jealous. He looked what he always looked. Too laid-back and handsome for *her* own good.

She was thinking of a suitable put-down when Mel, the sales executive from *Vitalis*, appeared behind them. Tory could guess why.

'Let me take those.' Lucas emptied Tory's hands of the maps, before observing, 'You've dropped something.'

'No, I haven't,' Tory was quick to deny and slower to catch on as he indicated a folded piece of paper on the floor.

'Well, someone has.' Mel bent to pick it up. 'A note, I'd say.'

The penny finally dropped as Tory snatched it from Mel's hand. 'It is mine, actually.'

'Okay, okay.' Mel held her hands up in mock defence. 'I wasn't going to read it. I can guess who it's from, though.'

Tory looked alarmed.

Lucas, however, kept his cool and lifted an enquiring brow. 'You can?'

'Well, I could be wrong—' Mel directed a hugely flirtatious smile at him '—but I'd lay money on it being our Features Editor, Richard. She's definitely caught his eye, haven't you, Tory?'

Under normal circumstances Tory would have objected. She didn't like her name being falsely linked with men. But she left it, relieved that Mel hadn't guessed the true source of the note.

He was still smiling, relaxed as ever, and when Mel began to engage him in conversation Tory took the chance to walk away.

She didn't open the note immediately. She suspected its contents would make her mad and she wanted to be alone when she read it. She didn't get that chance for a while as Tom Mackintosh, the head of the centre, rounded up the day with a little pep talk about the rationale behind the centre's courses before they were served a variety of night-time drinks back in the canteen. This time seating was less polarised with the winners of the champagne remaining vociferously bonded.

It was late when they all trooped off to dormitories. The washing facilities were limited and they took turns. Tory volunteered to go last and was locked in a shower cubicle when she finally unfolded his missive.

She expected it to offer an explanation for his appearance but it was frustratingly brief: 'TRY TO SLIP AWAY. NEED TO TALK. ROOM 12. L.'

While she showered, she debated her next actions. She had only a vague idea where Room Twelve might be—the male and female dormitories were on two different sides of a rectangle with staff rooms on the short side connecting the two. What if she crept along to the end, only to be witnessed going into his room?

She could hear Lucas's voice in her head, saying, So what? And, of course, he was right. According to her research, assignations were not uncommon on these management bonding weekends. Why should anyone conclude their meeting was anything other than this?

She could go now or she could wait till everyone slept and go later. She weighed the options up and decided on now, while she had the alibi of showering to account for her absence from her dormitory.

She quickly towelled herself dry, put on a pair of passion-killing winceyette pyjamas and stuffed her clothes and toilet bag in a cupboard to be retrieved later.

She padded down the corridor, ready with an excuse about looking for a drink if necessary. She discovered Room Twelve to be on the corner. She presumed he'd be expecting her and slipped inside, unannounced.

He was there, but not quite expecting her as he turned to face her, naked but for a towel tied loosely round the waist. From his wet hair it was evident he'd just come out of a shower.

She'd never seen him undressed before. Her eyes went from broad shoulders to a chest matted with dark hair tapering to towel level, and, beyond that, lean, muscular legs. She wasn't conscious of staring until he lifted a mocking brow, seeking her approval.

She should have ducked out of the room at that point. She wanted to. But behaving like an outraged virgin seemed pathetic under the circumstances.

So she stood her ground and, in chilly tones, said, 'You wanted to talk.'

Always perceptive, Lucas observed, 'You're mad with me, right?'

Hopping. But Tory opted for disdain. 'Mad? Why should I be mad? If you want to waste your time, checking up on me, not to mention putting the whole project in jeopardy, that's your business.'

'Mmm, I was afraid you'd see it that way.'

'There's another way?'

He grimaced at her sarcasm before explaining, 'Wiseman Global intended sending an observer to evaluate the course but their man dropped out at the eleventh hour. Chuck asked if I'd go instead. Nothing to do with Eastwich Productions. I apologise, however, if you feel undermined,' he added, almost verging on contrite.

Tory wondered if he really expected her to swallow such rot.

'If that's the case, why didn't you tell me on Wednesday when you phoned? You knew then, didn't you? Hence the "let's pretend we don't know each other" speech,' she recalled, lips twisting.

'Yes, well, I suppose I could have said something,' he conceded. 'To be honest, I was afraid you might not show.'

He gave her a long, steady, sincere look that had Tory questioning if she had the word 'gullible' tattooed on her forehead.

'And Mr Wiseman had no one else he could send?' she retorted smartly.

He hesitated, debating his answer. 'All right, you've got me. I throw in the towel.'

Not literally, Tory hoped, glancing involuntarily to his makeshift loincloth.

He read her mind and grinned slightly before continuing, 'Bad choice of phrase... Still, I admit it. Chuck has a band of yes-men only too happy to go fish for him. I volunteered solely so I could see you again, but, trust me, it had nothing to do with your work at Eastwich,' he ended on an intent note.

He had no need to say more. Tory raised her eyes to his and his gaze said it all. Her face suffused with warmth.

Lucas did nothing to hide his feelings. He'd had her and wanted her again. He wanted her enough to put up with a weekend of hard bunks and tepid showers.

He started to close the gap between them and Tory backed against the door.

'I've got to go,' she garbled out, alarmed by the racing of her own heart. 'They'll be wondering where I am.'

'I expect so,' he agreed with a slight smile.

He made no move to stop her, no move at all, but continued to look at her as if looking were enough.

Tory knew that her own feelings were the real danger. She had to get out of here. She felt the door handle pressing at her back. She just had to reach behind her and turn it.

But it seemed her limbs were paralysed. Even when he raised a hand to cup her cheek, she stood stock-still. Even when the hand shifted to caress her neck, she did nothing. The truth was she wanted this, needed it.

He drew her to him and she went. He began to lower his head to hers and she waited. He covered her mouth with his and finally freed her from passivity.

Still she didn't fight him but, moaning, parted her lips to

accept his kiss, to kiss him back, to taste him as he tasted her, exploring each other's mouths while hands explored each other's bodies.

This time both were stone-cold sober and the heat between them was spontaneous. Her hands slid over his bare back already slick with sweat, twined round the nape of his neck, buried into thick, wet hair while he pulled at her clothes, tugging free buttons to slip inside her pyjama top, seeking the swollen weight of her breasts. A thumb began to stroke and rub her nipple into throbbing life. She groaned aloud. He tore his mouth from hers. She fell back against the door. He pushed her top upwards, and bent to lick and suck on one pink bud of flesh until it ached. She grasped handfuls of his hair, forcing his head away, but only to offer her other peaked nipple to feed his hunger and hers.

When he started to push down the waistband of her pyjama trousers, she let him. She reached for him, too. He was already naked, the towel dislodged. She touched the hard pulse of his manhood and he exhaled deeply. She stroked along the thick shaft and drew pleasure from him as he groaned aloud. He let her touch him until his control began to slip, then he curved his hands under her hips and began to lift her upwards.

It took Tory a second or two to realise he meant to enter her, there, against the door. It took her another to accept that she wanted it, too, wanted him inside her. She put her arms round his shoulders and braced herself for that first loving thrust of sex.

It didn't happen. Wrapped round him, wrapped up in him, Tory had ceased to be aware of the outside world when a loud, ear-splitting ringing suddenly rent the air.

Dazed and uncomprehending in the first instant, she opened wide, alarmed eyes to Luc.

He was already up to speed, swearing aloud, 'Jesus, a fire drill!' as reality rudely interrupted their lovemaking.

Then everything happened in hurried reverse as Luc set her back on her feet and helped her to pull her pyjamas back on while footsteps ran up and down the corridors outside and doors, including their own, were rapped and a voice shouted with some urgency, 'Everybody out! This is not a drill! Everybody out!'

It was hard not to panic but it helped that Luc didn't. He had her dressed, with a warm jumper pulled over her head and a hurried instruction of, 'Go straight out!' in moments before he kissed her hard on the lips and pushed her out of the door.

It closed behind her. She knew she should be following the fleeing mass round her and understood that Luc would be out in the matter of seconds it took him to dress. But she just stood there, waiting for him.

It was one of the centre workers who took her arm and shouted above the uproar, 'For God's sake, get moving!'

He didn't give her any choice as he forcibly dragged her along the corridor to the fire exit at the end. He led her away from the house to join the others already marshalling on the driveway outside. She stood aloof from the group, watching the exit doors, and, when Luc failed to appear, she started walking back towards the building. Someone detained her, a hand grasping her arm. She tried to wrestle free but gave up as a familiar figure finally emerged from the fire exit.

Now dressed in jeans and sweatshirt, he strolled calmly from the building.

In that first instant of relief, Tory wanted to run and throw her arms about him. Fortunately relief was closely followed by sanity as she realised they were surrounded by witnesses. God alone knew if someone had already spotted her emerging from his room.

She turned round instead and walked away, suddenly unable to face him. She knew it was absurd. Five minutes earlier and they'd been about to have sex. She wouldn't call it making love. She couldn't. That took two. But here she now was, acting like a love-struck teenager.

She sought safety in numbers and clung to the crowd as heads were counted and explanations sought and finally given some time later by Tom Mackintosh. It seemed somebody had sneaked back to the day room to have a cigarette and, on finishing, had dropped the butt into a metal bin where it had ignited some waste paper. There had been no real danger, the fire contained within the bin, but enough smoke had been produced to trigger the alarms.

This information was greeted less than enthusiastically by the crowd, most standing shivering in night-wear, and accusing eyes scrutinised faces in the hope of identifying the guilty party.

Tory kept her eyes fixed to ground rather than risk catching Luc's eyes and was taken aback when Amanda Villiers declared, 'Well, far be it from me to go around accusing people, but you were absent for some time, Victoria, darling, weren't you?'

The 'darling' was as poisonous as Amanda's tone and Tory assumed no one would give her any credence but a glance round the others' faces told her otherwise.

At least Tory had the wit to say, 'I don't smoke.'

'So you say.' Amanda clearly didn't take her word as proof.

Tory was formulating another protest when she caught Luc's eye over Amanda's shoulder.

He raised a brow and Tory understood immediately. If she wanted, he would wade in and tell the group she'd been otherwise occupied.

She shook her head in horror. Bad enough that he'd discovered she was a sex maniac. She didn't want the rest of the world knowing it.

She was considering another line of defence when Mel spoke up, 'I saw Tory coming out of the shower room when the alarm went.'

'Mmm.' A sceptical sound from Amanda but she could hardly continue arguing and no one wanted to pursue it anyway when the all clear was given, allowing them to troop back inside.

Tory fell in step with Mel and, when she got the chance, mouthed the word, 'Thanks.'

'No problem.' Mel grinned back at her. 'I did actually see you coming out of a room, just not that one.'

She nodded towards Lucas, a few steps ahead of them.

Tory's face fell and she felt only a little better when Mel promised, 'Fast work—but don't worry, my lips are sealed.'

Of course it had been too much to hope that she hadn't been spotted, emerging from Luc's room. She supposed she should be grateful that Mel thought it a case of casual sex rather than conspiracy which had led Tory to his door.

Later, lying sleepless in her bunk, she wondered if subconsciously it *had* been her real reason to go calling on him. Yes, she'd wanted to know what he was up to. And true, she had been incensed at the idea he was checking on her. But it hadn't taken much for her to suspend hostilities and re-enact their last encounter. And if the fire bell had saved her from going the whole way, she'd surely been willing.

She cringed now when she considered *how* willing. It was as if she'd turned into a different person. With other men, she'd been in control, choosing where and when and how they made love. With Lucas, no thinking or planning went into it. It seemed he just had to touch her and she wanted him. She didn't need words or tender gestures from him. She didn't care how he took her, as long as he did. Passion overwhelmed everything else.

And there was no point in saying she wouldn't let him next time, because she knew she would. No way of her dismissing it as 'just sex', because it wasn't. Ordinary sex, even loving sex with Charlie had never been like that.

It was a need, a hunger, a desperate thing. She still wanted him now. Only pride stopped her slipping out of the dormitory and walking the few yards down to his room.

Pride told her that, for him, she was simply a minor distraction. He was a man who worked hard and consequently played hard. Sex was sport to him, one he happened to be good at, perhaps through practice. Love was something else, quite unconnected.

And she had to give it to him. He never used the word love, never pretended. Right from the beginning, it had been a matter of sex. He hadn't wasted time wining or dining her, impressing her or persuading her. From week one he'd asked her to leave Alex and move in with him. But it had always been clear that sex was the driving force.

So why not go along for the ride? She asked herself that

now as she lay on her bunk, knees drawn up, trying to ignore the ache of longing inside her.

She didn't have to think too hard for the answer. She'd never used the word either. Love. But she'd thought it.

And what if the ache didn't go away? What if it got worse each time they made love? What if it consumed her?

CHAPTER TEN

THINGS were meant to look different in the morning and, yes, when Tory woke to the sound of Amanda grumbling, the previous night took on an air of unreality. She felt tired and irritable rather than frustrated or lovesick as she yawned herself awake and joined the lengthy queue for the centre's temperamental plumbing.

By the time she'd queued for breakfast, she was testy enough to resist any overture.

Not that Luc made any. Tory only knew he was present because, *en route* to her table, she'd briefly caught his eye. He looked as he always did—amused by something, or maybe just life. He certainly showed no signs of regret for his behaviour last night.

Tory looked away quickly and deliberately sat on a bench with her back to him. That was how she planned getting through the rest of the weekend. By ignoring him totally.

That wasn't so easy, of course. He was there ostensibly to observe, and observe he did. Every time she looked round, he seemed to be in view, smiling even when she blanked him.

She was just glad that she was reasonably fit and didn't end up a gasping, sobbing heap in the middle of the centre's assault course like Angela, the sales director from *Toi*. Or be as scared of heights as Sam, and be pressured into abseiling down a cliff-face, only to go catatonic halfway down and have to be rescued by centre staff.

In fact Tory acquitted herself reasonably well in such physical challenges but that hardly endeared her to Amanda who became increasingly vituperative. Tory was careful to react minimally. She wanted no suggestion that she'd encouraged Amanda's frothing at the mouth for the camera.

In fact, Tory was surprised how outspoken most of the

course members were, considering they knew they were being filmed. Even if Tom Mackintosh hadn't announced it at the beginning, the CCTV cameras were easy to spot. But it seemed, after some initial reticence, people just forgot about them.

They were more wary of Lucas himself, watching from the sidelines.

'Who do you think the KGB is working for, then?' speculated Jackie, *Vitalis*'s art director, during team games that evening.

'KGB?' was echoed by Mel.

Jackie nodded towards Luc. 'Killingly Gorgeous Bloke.'

It raised some laughter before Mel suggested, 'Ask Tory.'

Curious eyes fixed on Tory and she actually felt herself go red as she muttered back, 'How should I know?'

Mel grinned mischievously but didn't pursue it; perhaps she remembered Tory had helped her out twice that afternoon when they'd been doing daft things in canoes.

'He keeps watching you,' another girl put in. 'I noticed that when we were abseiling.'

'That's what he's here to do,' Tory pointed out.

'No, *you* specifically,' she added.

'Lucky thing,' rejoined Jackie. 'I certainly wouldn't kick him out of bed.'

Neither would Tory. That was the problem.

Listening to other opinions confirmed what Tory already suspected. Lucas was too popular for his own good—or for hers.

She shrugged, a pretence of indifference, and was relieved when they returned to the task, making a mock-up format for a new magazine. As ideas began to flow and rivalries were set aside, it proved an enjoyable exercise and there was much jubilation in the group when their creation was declared the winner.

They were sitting together later, toasting each other with their prize of champagne, when Lucas and some other staff came to sit alongside, offering them congratulations. By studiously staring into her glass, Tory gave him no openings to address her directly. She knew it might seem childish but she was scared of betraying any emotion.

He, of course, was as relaxed as ever. When Jackie specifically asked him if he worked for the centre or Wiseman Global, he stated neither and, without telling any explicit lies, gave the impression that he was an interested outsider, considering running his own management course.

'Well, darling,' Jackie continued in her flamboyant style, 'if you omit the assault course, abseiling and cold showers, and fill it with hunky, available men like yourself, we'll definitely sign up, won't we, girls?'

This was greeted with general laughter and agreement.

Tory remained aloof but a surreptitious glance confirmed that Lucas wasn't in the least bit disconcerted at being centre of attention.

'I'm honoured by the compliment, ladies,' he drawled back, 'though, the truth is, I'm no longer available.'

A mock groan went round the table while Tory's eyes flew involuntarily to his. He caught the surprise in them and slanted her a smile.

'You're married?' Jackie concluded.

He shook his head. 'Not yet.'

'But considering it?' she added.

He made a balancing motion with his right hand, as if marriage might or might not be on the agenda.

'Who is she, then?' asked Mel.

The same question was burning its way through Tory's brain. Not once had he hinted there was someone else in the background, someone he was serious about.

He glanced towards her once more and, catching the daggers look she was sending, answered circumspectly, 'I can't really say at the moment.'

Tory understood. He meant he didn't dare say. It made her even angrier. Did he imagine she had so little dignity she'd fight over him?

Jackie and the others remained intrigued. 'Is she married?'

'Not to my knowledge,' he replied.

'Someone famous?'

'A model?'

'On TV?'

The suggestions came thick and fast and he scotched them with a brief laugh. 'No, nothing like that. She's just a very private person who wouldn't appreciate me telling the world about her. Especially when I haven't worked up courage yet to tell her how I feel.'

This news was greeted with a collective sigh as the rest obviously viewed him as that increasingly rare type of man— a romantic.

Tory was left biting her tongue in preference to making a scene by denouncing him as the faithless cheat she now knew he was.

When someone asked him, 'What's she like, then?' Tory couldn't sit through any more. Scraping back her chair, she muttered to Mel about being tired and, before she could hear anything about Lucas's other girl, she walked away.

She took refuge in her dormitory and was lying on her bunk, trying and failing to concentrate on a novel, when Mel appeared.

'You okay?' Mel asked.

'Fine,' she answered shortly.

'I just wondered—' Mel hesitated before taking the plunge '—you seemed a little upset when Luc was talking about his girl.'

'*Upset?*' echoed Tory as if she'd never felt such an emotion in her life. 'Why should I be upset?'

'No reason,' Mel pacified, 'except that after last night—'

'Nothing happened last night!' denied Tory, as much to herself as Mel. 'You may have seen me coming out of his room—'

'No *may* about it.'

'But it was not what you think.'

'No?' Mel raised a sceptical brow.

'No!' denied Tory in resounding tones.

'So you won't mind hearing about his other girl, then?' Mel challenged.

Tory wondered why Mel was determined to twist the knife.

'I couldn't care less,' she claimed.

It wasn't true, of course. Half of her wanted to hear, the other half wanted to scream.

Mel continued determinedly, 'Apparently she's a bit younger than him. Quiet but strong-willed and fairly bright. Sporty. Not very glamorous. More your girl-next-door type. Lovely, though, with a really good complexion and large, soulful eyes.'

The description didn't strike any chords with Tory but why should it? He was hardly going to go out of his way to introduce one girlfriend to another.

Not that *she* was a girlfriend. From recollection he'd never even asked her out—asking her to sleep with him wasn't the same.

'Sound like anyone you know?' added Mel at her silence.

'Why should it?' Tory echoed aloud. 'I mean… I've just met the man.'

Mel looked at her in wide-eyed disbelief.

Tory suddenly wondered if she and Luc had been sussed.

But, no, Mel just went on to shake her head and mutter, 'A case of self-induced blindness, if you want my opinion.'

Tory gave her a quizzical look, as Mel grabbed a towel and wash bag to beat the rush to the shower room.

Later, when she should have been asleep, Tory dwelled over the attributes of Lucas's lady love, as relayed via Mel, and became increasingly convinced that he'd been making it all up as he'd gone along. She remembered the half-smile he'd been wearing when he'd begun his 'true confessions'. She knew that smile, had seen it before. It was the smile that said life was a joke.

And that, she suspected, was what he'd been playing on the others—spinning out a yarn about a fictitious girlfriend to keep them at a distance.

Or could it be the opposite? Tory recalled the women's faces at his tale of romantic love, their wistful expressions at this rare breed of man who was not only handsome and sexy, but true and faithful in character. Was Lucas astute enough to realise just how desirable that made him seem? Even as he'd claimed to be unavailable, had he been casting a net to see if he could land another gullible idiot like herself?

Because that was what she was. She could pretend to be experienced, even convince herself that she knew the score, but leave her alone with Lucas for a minute and she was as easy to take in as a schoolgirl.

She had to face it. A few tender looks from him, a passionate kiss or two, and her heart was racing as if it were true love, when it really was just sex. She only realised afterwards, but by then it was too late.

Best thing was to keep away from him altogether and she managed it at breakfast the next morning which was then followed by a briefing on the day's main event, a ten-mile-round hike and treasure hunt for real. But he was waiting his moment, catching her as she went down to collect some supplies from the kitchen.

'Look, Tory—' he brought her to a halt '—about the other night...'

Tory didn't want to listen. 'Someone's coming,' she hissed at him, simply to get free.

They heard footfalls, making her lie the truth, but he didn't react as she'd hoped. Instead he pulled her inside the nearest room, an empty office.

Tory wrested her arm away, complaining, 'You're going to blow my cover.'

'I don't care,' he dismissed. 'Sorting out things between us is more important.'

'Well, *I* care,' she retorted angrily, 'and I'm the one about to go on a ten-mile hike with these people. If anything happens, I want to be able to trust them.'

His eyes narrowed. 'What do you mean—if anything happens?'

Tory wasn't exactly sure. She just had a bad feeling about this particular exercise.

'Nothing,' she discounted at length. 'Look, I have to go. The minibus will be waiting to take us to the start point.'

She reached for the door handle and he put a hand on her arm once more. 'Meet me when you get back, then?'

'There won't be time,' she pointed out. 'After the debriefing, we have to drive back to London.'

'I could take you,' he offered.

Tory shook her head. 'I have to go on the minibus to get feedback.'

She was still taking this project seriously even if he clearly wasn't.

'Okay,' he conceded, 'so I'll follow you down and meet you off the bus.'

He was obviously determined and Tory was tired of arguing. She settled for saying, 'Won't *she* mind?'

'*She?*'

'The girl you were telling Mel and the others about.'

His blank look changed to a surprised, then amused one. 'Oh, that girl.'

For a man caught out, he showed no signs of guilt.

'Unless of course you made her up,' Tory suggested tartly.

He raised a quizzical brow. 'Why should I have done that?'

'Who knows?' She no longer did.

'Well, no, she's real enough,' he confessed, grinning slightly, 'but there's no reason to be jealous—'

'*Jealous?*' Tory cut across him, pride surfacing. 'Me? You think I'm jealous?'

'I didn't actually say that.' He raised his hands in a pacifying gesture.

But Tory didn't wish to be pacified. Much safer to be angry, disdainful.

'Why should I be jealous?' she challenged and, before he might actually answer, ran on rashly, 'I have Alex, remember?'

The words were out before she realised quite what she was saying.

Mr Laid-back suddenly turned into Mr Uptight, grating, 'Alex?'

'Yes.' It was too late to backtrack even if she wanted to.

His eyes narrowed to slits. 'So, tell me, do you happen to know where Alex is this weekend?'

Tory frowned at the question. She did know the answer. Alex was in Edinburgh, trying to patch things up with his wife. But why had Lucas asked such a thing?

Unless he knew, too.

'Do you?' she countered.

She watched his face, the changing expressions, and guessed he did. She waited for him to throw it in her face—that her live-in lover was with someone else.

He opened his mouth to speak, then closed it, shaking his head.

Tory understood. On the brink of exposing Alex, he had decided against it. But why?

Perhaps it suited him—that she maintain some kind of relationship with Alex. It would justify him playing the field in turn.

'Forget it.' He finally opened the door, allowing her to leave.

Tory escaped but with a heavy heart. Why had she mentioned Alex? It made all her other earlier denials seem so many lies.

Pride, she supposed. She hadn't wanted him to think her jealous. Forget that she was—achingly, gnawingly, spectacularly—at the idea of him with some other girl.

She felt like a schoolgirl again, in love for the first time. Only she never had been. Not with Charlie or anybody else. She finally understood that. Because love wasn't the warm, pleasant feeling she'd imagined it was.

She caught the drift of her thoughts and brought herself up sharply. She had to stop this. What she felt for Lucas wasn't love either. It couldn't be. She wouldn't let it be. It was desire, pure and simple, or maybe more accurately lust, less pure but just as simple.

So why didn't she let it burn itself out? Good question. Why didn't she just give way to sexual longing and climb into bed with Lucas the very next opportunity and stay there until the fire was out?

She knew the answer. She was scared, that was why. But she resisted analysing her fear.

She didn't get a chance, anyway, as she collected the supplies and headed for the bus to find her team already boarded and waiting.

Her team? Well, not quite hers. Or even a team. Five of them. Should have been six but it seemed Jessica Parnell, the senior editor from *Vitalis*, had woken up that morning and decided life was too short to scramble over hillsides to hold on to a job she had loathed for at least the last two years. Having had this revealing thunderbolt, she had shared it in no uncertain terms with Tom Mackintosh before calling a minicab to take her to the nearest railway station.

Mel shared it second-hand as they were driven to their drop-off point.

Amanda almost purred with satisfaction. Her dismissal of, 'Bloody prima donna,' however, was too much for Carl, their advertising sales director.

Normally an anything-for-a-quiet-life type, he actually commented aloud, 'Takes one to know one.'

'I beg your pardon,' demanded Amanda with an imperious look.

For once Carl wasn't quelled. 'You heard.'

She'd heard but evidently she didn't believe it. Amanda really wasn't used to opposition. It left her fuming with silent indignation.

To Tory, it was probably the most interesting aspect of the weekend. At the office Amanda ruled *Toi* with an iron fist in an iron glove and had expected to do so at the centre, too. But gradually, as various tasks challenged people's perceptions of themselves—or possibly fatigue and irritability set in—fewer and fewer of *Toi*'s staff were prepared to dance to Amanda's discordant tune. Tory was almost sorry she couldn't return to the office to see if this defiance would continue.

Amanda now complained loudly to Lucy, the somewhat sheepish make-up editor from *Vitalis*, going as far as suggesting that some people were in for a rude awakening on Monday morning, while Carl started to sing loudly and Mel grinned, seemingly enjoying the internecine strife.

So, no, they were not a team, which increased Tory's niggling worry as they were dumped in the middle of nowhere with basic supplies, a compass, one map and a series of clues as to what landmarks they had to capture with the digital camera they were issued.

They had practised map-reading, of course, and each team had a so-called expert. Carl was theirs and did seem to know what he was doing, although from their first step in what was hopefully the right direction Amanda tried to undermine him.

Despite this, they managed to follow the right track, finding the 'bridge over troubled water', a tiny footbridge over a fast hill stream, 'Stonehenge' or a mini version of stone slabs and columns, and 'the last resting place' which turned out to be a couple of wooden crosses in what had been the back garden of an old shepherd's hut on a hill. The names Rover and Robbie could faintly be seen, etched out of the wood. Dogs, they assumed.

They rested there for lunch: beans and sausage cooked over a Primus stove. Amanda, needless to say, slated such food but she still ate her share.

They were well over halfway and beginning to feel good about themselves when the rain started. At first it wasn't heavy and they walked on, quickening their pace slightly, but then it began to come straight down, almost in sheets. On open moorland, with nowhere to shelter, they pressed on. No bitching or complaining now. Breath was saved to battle the elements.

Even Amanda kept going, but she was clearly suffering, with chafing boots and tired legs, and when they were walking along the edge of a slight incline she tripped and rolled. She didn't have far to fall. Tory scrambled down after her in seconds. But Amanda's groans sounded genuine enough and she shrieked as Tory touched her leg, trying to find the source of her injuries.

It seemed she'd smashed her knee against rock as she'd tumbled. How serious, it was hard to tell. No one wanted to peel off clothing in this downpour. But their first attempt to support Amanda to her feet and walk warned them it wasn't a simple sprain.

It was Tory who said, 'We'll have to use the CB to call in.'

Carl was reluctant. 'We'll lose if we do that.'

Tory stared at him in disbelief. 'For God's sake, Carl. The game is over. She's really hurt!' she almost shouted the words at him.

He looked resentful but took out the CB handset from his bag. No amount of fiddling with bands and aerials, however, produced anything more than static. Either it was malfunctioning or the storm had broken up the signal.

Various suggestions followed and were rejected. They could sit and wait for rescue but Carl admitted he'd deviated from their suggested route, opting for a shorter but steeper path, and it could be hours until they were located. Hostile glares were sent in Carl's direction but no one commented aloud. They still had to rely on him to get them back.

Another attempt was made to shoulder Amanda's weight between Carl and Tory. With no alternative, Amanda gritted her teeth and tried to bear it, but the occasional sob still escaped from her. It was hard not to jar her leg and their progress was painfully slow.

Tory wasn't sure they should even be moving Amanda and was relieved when they finally came upon potential shelter. 'Over there in the rock.'

It was more an indentation than a cave, with barely space for two, but they carefully lowered Amanda to the ground while they took stock. It was decided that someone should stay with Amanda while the rest walked back to the centre.

Before anyone volunteered, Amanda spoke up. 'Victoria...I'd like Victoria to stay.'

Tory was taken aback. She'd imagined Amanda would prefer just about anyone else.

She glanced down at Amanda and was awarded an almost pleading look.

'Well?' Carl prompted her for a decision.

'Fine,' conceded Tory with good grace and joked weakly, 'as long as we get the rest of the chocolate.'

'You deserve it.' Mel gave her a commiserating smile and dug out a foil space blanket and torch to hand over before the rest of the party moved on.

Tory tried to make Amanda more comfortable, propping her against a makeshift pillow of their rucksacks before draping the blanket over her. They were already very wet and the wind whipped some of the rain into their shelter, but Tory did her best to shield Amanda from it.

They didn't talk much at first but Tory finally gave way to curiosity. 'Why did you want me to stay? I mean, we haven't exactly hit it off.'

Amanda pulled a face, conceding the point, then said by way of explanation, 'That Mel character loathes me and, as for Lucy, she's such a wimp.'

'So I'm it by default,' Tory concluded dryly.

'Perhaps,' admitted Amanda in a similar tone.

Well, it was honest. Tory had to give her that. She was also quite surprised by how well Amanda was behaving in the circumstances. She was clearly in pain yet now she had something real to complain about she was almost stoical.

'How long do you think before we're rescued?' was all she asked.

'Hard to say.' Tory didn't want to hold out any false promises.

'They may struggle to find us,' added Amanda.

That possibility had occurred to Tory but it seemed important to stay upbeat. 'I think Carl pretty much knows our location on the map.'

Amanda nodded, then commented, 'God, Jessica will be laughing her socks off when she hears about this.'

'Jessica?'

'Jessica Parnell—*Vitalis*'s senior editor. She was right. What the hell are we doing, playing girl scouts at our age?'

'You're not that old,' Tory protested automatically.

Of course she should have known the older woman would come back with, 'How old do you imagine I am?'

Thirty-eight was Tory's guess so she took off five years and said, 'Thirty-three.'

'I wish,' responded Amanda, obviously pleased. But not pleased enough to reveal her real age. Instead she said, 'I've been in the business more than twenty years. It really is true about time, you know, it flies.'

There was more than a hint of regret in Amanda's tone, even a suggestion of vulnerability, but Tory wondered if they weren't just products of their current situation.

'One moment you're the hottest thing in town,' continued Amanda, 'the next you're abseiling down a bloody cliff, just to survive…and what do you have to show for it?'

The question might have been rhetorical but Tory couldn't resist answering, 'A wardrobe full of designer clothes, the chicest of sports coupés and probably a garden flat in Hampstead.'

'Notting Hill, actually—' Amanda smiled briefly '—and, yes, I admit there are compensations… Just don't go thinking they're enough.'

It seemed like well-intentioned advice but Tory wasn't used to that from Amanda. 'Why are you telling me all this?'

Amanda caught her suspicious glance and read it astutely, 'You mean when I'm normally acting like the editor from hell?'

'Something like that.' Tory was surprised by the other woman's self-awareness.

'I'm not sure.' Amanda thought about it before coming up with, 'Maybe I see myself in you if I roll back the film fifteen years.'

Tory managed not to look horrified, although she couldn't imagine herself turning out like Amanda under any circumstances.

'In fact, I'm willing to bet we come from similar backgrounds,' Amanda went on. 'Raised by a single mother. High rise flat in inner-city London. State school. And a burning desire for something better.'

Tory could have denied it. It wasn't an exact blueprint of her early life. But it was close enough.

'Is that so wrong?' she said at length.

'Not at all,' Amanda replied, 'but knowing what you *don't* want out of life isn't the same as knowing what you do. And by the time you work it out, it might already be too late.'

'So what do *you* want?' Tory wasn't convinced Amanda was being genuine.

'In the short term, out of this hole,' Amanda said with a grimace. 'In the long term, what all us career girls really secretly desire—man, home, family.'

For a moment Tory didn't react. She was waiting for one of Amanda's biting, sarcastic laughs to follow. But nothing.

Instead she ran on, 'You can deny that, if you want. I certainly did for years, then one day you wake up and smell the roses. Only by that time, they've all gone—the nice young men who would have married you. And the bastards, the ones you really wanted, they've started to settle down, too, but with younger models,' she finished on a note more rueful than bitter.

Tory didn't know what to say. Not in a million years would she have suspected that an unhappy woman, frustrated by childlessness and loneliness, lay under Amanda's usual diamond-hard exterior. She felt an impulse to comfort but didn't think Amanda would accept it—not even in her current state.

Still, she felt the need to give something back, something of herself, as she finally responded, 'It's hard not to envy people sometimes. I had a boyfriend once—a fiancé, actually. It didn't work out and he went on to marry someone else and have kids. I met him again recently and I suppose I felt envy, but it turned out they weren't as happy as they seemed.'

'Most couples aren't happy,' Amanda observed in return. 'Not truly, deeply, deliriously. Not all the time. But maybe it's enough not to be *un*happy.'

Tory wasn't sure she agreed. 'I think being married and having kids for the sake of it would ultimately make a person more unhappy than being on their own.'

'So speaks a twenty-something-year-old,' Amanda opined. 'See how you feel at forty, assuming you're still alone.'

Tory heard the note of self-pity in Amanda's voice and did wonder if it would be any different for her.

Chances were she'd still be alone.

Not that she saw herself pining for Lucas Ryecart for the rest of her life. There would be other men. Perhaps not quite as attractive or smart. Nor as sexually exciting. But would she want another relationship that was both so intense and so basically shallow again?

Yet there was no point wanting it all—husband, children, home, happy-ever-afters. No point in wanting what she couldn't have.

Maybe she was luckier than Amanda, knowing it wasn't possible, knowing it would be crying for the moon.

She didn't feel lucky, however.

Didn't look it either as Amanda remarked, 'Well, now I've depressed the hell out of both of us, can you think of a way of passing another four hours?'

Intended to raise a smile, Tory managed a weak one before suggesting with irony, 'I-spy?'

'Riveting,' Amanda applauded. 'Bags I start.'

It was as good a way as any to pass time. They followed it with a game of name the film, twenty questions and their choice of desert island discs.

As time dragged and the storm failed to let up, they both began to shiver from cold and gradually lost any enthusiasm for anything but waiting.

An hour became two, then three and Amanda fell into an uneasy sleep, jerking with each inadvertent movement of her bad leg. Tory watched over her, growing concerned that they might have to spend a night outdoors. The rain had ceased some time ago but the temperature was still unseasonably low and she wondered how cold did it need to be before hypothermia set in.

She tried distracting herself from that possibility by planning her documentary of the weekend. She would splice between the staff's lectures and worthy intentions, and the reality of how much ''team-building'' and ''attitude-changing'' had been effected. Being lost on the moor would give it more dramatic impact, as proof of the centre's poor safety procedures and too exacting demands, but she would be reluctant to use it as a sign of retribution for Amanda, even if she had bitched her way through the weekend.

It was curious to think that underneath Amanda's tough exterior lay deep insecurities. Tory supposed it was the same for most people—a side they showed the world, and a side they kept secret.

Well, maybe not everyone. Involuntarily her thoughts went to Lucas. He seemed remarkably straightforward in his approach to life. He saw something he wanted, he went after it and made no apologies for the fact.

Tory wished in some ways she could emulate him. Be more ruthless, or at least more honest. After he'd tried—and pretty much succeeded—in seducing her on Friday, she'd cut him dead. Yet the truth was she'd loved it. She'd loved every second of those five desperate minutes with Luc. It had only been afterwards that she'd felt bad, seeing her easy surrender as weakness and resolving to resist the next time.

Now she wondered whether it would be simpler just to give in, to accept they were going to have a relationship and let it run its course. It would be brief. How could it be otherwise? Neither of them could commit. But if they both went into it with their eyes wide open, where was the harm?

Tory was still debating the issue when she heard it. A blessed sound. At first dismissed as imagination. How could she hear a car engine when there wasn't a road for miles? But that was what it was, or more precisely they were: four-by-fours, revving up and down gears as they tackled the terrain for which they were built.

Tory shook Amanda gently awake, then scrambled to her own feet, intending to go in the direction of the sound. Only hours of sheltering in one spot combined with wet clothing resulted in a debilitating cramp that had her collapsing back to the ground in agony.

They heard the engines cut and for an awful moment both women had visions of their rescuers searching in the wrong spot before abandoning them. It was with immense relief that they heard the voices drawing nearer.

Neither could now move but they could cry out, which they proceeded to do until they were hoarse from shouting and the first figure appeared through the clearing beyond them.

It was the abseiling coach from the centre, closely followed by three other men.

Tory had eyes for only one of them and he had eyes for only her as he dropped to his knees beside her. 'Are you all right?'

All right? She was absolutely marvellous. They had come. *He* had come.

'Your leg?' Lucas guessed.

Tory realised she was still massaging it. 'It's just cramp. Almost past. Amanda's hurt, though.'

'The medic's taking care of her.'

Tory glanced towards the little group round Amanda. A man she didn't recognise was already cutting off her trouser leg to examine the knee. Carl, their map-reader, had come, too, and was holding a folded stretcher.

'Can you walk?' Lucas added to her.

'I think so.' She let him put an arm round her shoulders and help her to her feet. Her calf muscle protested but she limped a couple of steps before finding herself being literally swept off her feet.

He told the others he was taking her back, then picked his way carefully over the rough terrain, easing them down a slight slope to where the two vehicles were.

He slid her into the rear bench seat. Her rucksack was on the floor. A pair of clean jeans, T-shirt and sweatshirt lay on the bench seat beside her.

'You'd better take off your wet clothes,' he instructed.

She nodded and shivered but didn't seem to have the energy.

He looked askance at her before saying, 'This isn't some clever plan to get you undressed, you know.'

'I know,' she echoed through shattering teeth. Reaction had set in and she felt cold to the bone.

'I'll get the heater on.' He went round to the driver's side to switch on the engine and heaters, before climbing into the back with her.

'Come on, trust me.' He unzipped her jacket. 'I promise I'll behave like a gentleman.'

Tory didn't need this reassurance. She didn't resist as he

slipped off her jacket, then outer layers of damp garments, before helping her into the dry clothes.

'You stay in the back—' he strapped her in '—and try to rest while I drive you home.'

Tory wasn't sure where he meant by home—the centre, the hotel in London or back to Norwich.

'Can we wait?' she asked as he slipped behind the driver's wheel. 'See if Amanda's all right.'

'Yes, okay,' he agreed with some reluctance. 'I'll just turn.'

It took several minutes to manoeuvre the vehicle to face the way he'd come and by that time the others had appeared, carrying Amanda on the stretcher.

Tory could see her knee had been bandaged and she watched as the men carefully eased her into the bench seat of the other off-roader.

'Where are they going to take her?' she asked Lucas as he waved a hand at the others and pulled away.

'Nearest hospital, I imagine. We can telephone the centre later,' he promised. 'For now, I suggest you hang on.'

Tory did just that as the vehicle bumped over the rough terrain and she was jolted to and fro.

It took them almost half an hour to reach what could be described as a road. Even then it was a minor one. Tory tried and failed to work out if they were going east to Norwich or south to London, but she didn't really care. The warmth of the car was lulling her into a state of drowsiness and she didn't fight it. She rested her head against the window and was asleep by the time they reached main roads.

London was her last waking thought but she was wrong.

When she woke, she was too disorientated to know where she was until Lucas came round to help her down to the street outside her flat in Norwich.

She was glad. She wasn't really injured but felt weak and shivery and home seemed the best place to recover.

He shouldered her rucksack, and, with a hand at her elbow, supported her up the steps to the front door. By chance she'd taken her house keys with her to Derby and he dug them out of one of the side pockets. He tried both keys before identifying the correct one, then used the other on her inner door.

Entering the flat, Tory was relieved to find the lights off, suggesting that Alex had yet to return. She could just about cope with this new solicitous Lucas but she suspected the old one was lurking somewhere, ready to emerge if Alex appeared.

As it was, Alex had left enough pointers to his presence. Tory felt tired just surveying the mess of take-away cartons, clothes and books.

'I take it you didn't leave the place like this,' Lucas concluded from her disgruntled expression. 'I'm amazed you put up with it.'

'And you're Mr Clean and Tidy, I suppose,' she snapped rather childishly, resenting the criticism.

'No, but I'm not a slob.' His gaze rested on a pair of male underpants actually lying on the sofa.

Tory wrinkled her nose, wondering if they were dirty or not, and resolved to give Alex his marching orders as soon as possible.

'Well, thanks for the lift,' she said before Lucas could make any further comment.

She imagined he'd be dying to get away to his nice clean room at Abbey Lodge.

He ignored her, however, saying, 'You can't have eaten since lunch. I'll make you something.'

'It's all right—' a surprised Tory turned down the offer '—I just want to rest.'

'You have to eat a little,' he insisted. 'Slip into bed and I'll bring you tea and toast.'

'I doubt there's any bread,' she countered dryly. 'Alex doesn't shop.'

She made the comment without thinking.

It almost begged a sarcastic reply. He didn't disappoint, drawling back, 'I wonder what Alex actually does do... On seconds thoughts, don't tell me.'

It could have been a joke but his eyes said not. They narrowed to a point.

'Please don't...' Tory didn't finish the appeal.

He understood, though, switching back to brisk concern. 'Okay, go rest and I'll forage in the kitchen.'

Tory hesitated. She didn't have the energy to keep arguing with him but neither did she have the energy for another bedroom scene with this man.

'Don't worry, you'll be safe.' He read her with irritating accuracy. 'Sharing another man's bed doesn't appeal to me.'

Tory felt her face go red. It was absurd because she had nothing to feel guilty or embarrassed about.

'Ten minutes—' he gave her a gentle push in the direction of the bedroom door '—and I'll expect you tucked up in bed with your teddy and a long-sleeved nightgown buttoned to the throat.'

This time he *was* joking but Tory picked up the underlying message. She had nothing to worry about.

She switched to asking, 'Could you phone the centre about Amanda?'

'Yeah, sure,' he agreed easily. 'Now go on.'

She went through to her bedroom and, with some relief, saw no sign of Alex in the room. At least he had respected her privacy this far.

She undressed quickly, choosing a nightie that, though short, was suitably unglamorous, and climbed into bed, all the time wondering if she should tell him the truth. That Alex did nothing, was nothing. But would he believe such an admission?

She worried the thought round in her head but came to no conclusion before her eyes became too heavy to keep open and she let it all go.

Lucas put the tray he brought down on a chest of drawers and sat for a while on a wicker chair, watching over her. She seemed much younger in sleep and more vulnerable, but he supposed it was an illusion. She certainly had proved herself one of the toughest on the weekend's course.

He recalled his reaction when her party had returned. He'd been waiting for them, of course—waiting for her. They'd been hours late. He'd already insisted the centre call up a search party when they'd finally trooped in, wet and miserable, one of the women breaking down in sobs.

He'd been furious when he'd heard their story. Having abandoned Tory and Amanda, they had lost their bearings for a while and even wasted half an hour taking shelter themselves before continuing. The girl called Mel had tried to reassure him that Tory was fine but it had made no difference. All he'd been able to think of was Tory, her unruly mop of hair plastered wet against a face pinched with cold and her slight figure, drenched and huddling somewhere out there in the dark. He'd joined the rescue mission in his own off-roader, meeting the centre's opposition with a threat to sue if any harm had come to Tory.

His reaction seemed over-dramatic now. She had been in no real danger. She'd kept her head and waited for rescue—exactly as she should have done. But he hadn't been thinking straight; what had been happening to Tory had somehow got mixed up in his head with the accident in which he'd lost Jessica, his first wife.

Not quite the same. Jessica had died in a car crash. There had been nothing anyone could have done, least of all him. He'd been on the other side of the world. But it had still felt like a rerun—as if he'd been going to next see Tory lying on some cold mortuary slab.

He shook his head, a dismissive gesture. He wasn't a man given to premonitions and if this had been one it was way off base. Nevertheless he recognised the emotion involved—a fear of loss.

Not that he had Tory to lose. Not yet, anyway.

CHAPTER ELEVEN

TORY woke in the night to find Lucas asleep on her wicker bedroom chair. She watched him for a while as he had watched her. It was odd: most people looked relaxed in sleep. Lucas was different—he was tense and restless, as if bad things were happening in his dreams.

She watched until she found she couldn't bear it any longer. She didn't consider her next action as she slid out of the bed and came round to his side. She knew not to waken him too suddenly. She put a gentle hand on the nape of his neck, the other on his hand and exerted the faintest pressure.

She thought he would gradually come awake but he reacted instantly, shuddering at her touch and issuing a brief startled cry.

Tory might have retreated but he caught her hand in a hard, almost convulsive grip. Only when he jerked his head back and opened his eyes to see what had woken him did he ease his hold.

Tory wasn't scared. She saw a range of emotions, dread, relief, shame, flitting across his handsome face before the usual mask slotted back in place.

'Bad dream. Sorry.' He finally managed a lazy smile behind which to hide.

But Tory wasn't fooled. 'You get them often, don't you?' She didn't know how she knew this. She just did.

He shrugged. 'Not really.'

Tory took that as a yes.

'Things you've seen?'

'Partly.'

It was a brief admission. Tory didn't press him further. If he wanted to tell her more, he would.

'I should be going,' was what he said now.

But he made no move. Perhaps he couldn't. She was standing too close.

And Tory didn't want to take a step back because she'd finally accepted. This man was her fate, for good or ill. She was tired of running from it.

She looked at him with solemn, unswerving eyes. She wanted him to take her, cover her body with the hard heat of his, be gentle, be rough, control her, possess her, but ultimately love her. She longed for it even as she acknowledged that loving this man might destroy her—especially if he couldn't love her back.

Lucas held her gaze and understood. Not totally. But enough to know she'd surrendered herself to an inevitability he'd recognised from the beginning. Him and her. Together.

He took her hand and drew her gently down. He put an arm round her waist. She was soft and warm and yielding. His desire for her was immediate but this time he didn't want to rush things.

He waited for her to make the first move. She did so tentatively, a finger tracing the small scar that puckered the corner of an eyelid. Then, braving rejection, she cupped his face with her hands and put her mouth to his.

It was the lightest of kisses, her dry lips on his. Chaste but somehow sexy, too. He had to stop himself kissing her back.

Tory wasn't discouraged by his lack of response. She understood, too. This time she had to make the running, do the seducing.

It wasn't going to be hard. His hands had already left her waist to curve round her hips and his lower body shifted against her in arousal.

She threaded her fingers into his thick dark hair until she could pull back his head slightly and once more put her mouth to his, only this time she slid the tip of her tongue between his lips, moistening them. She withdrew immediately, however, when he began to kiss her back and nuzzled teasingly at his neck, twining her arms round, softly licking and tasting his skin, biting his earlobe with gentle savagery until she felt him draw several deep, unsteady breaths. Then she slid her mouth back to his and stole his breath and his reason as she kissed him with unfettered passion.

Lucas's resolve to take things slowly broke like glass shattering as he thrust his tongue inside her sweet, moist mouth and she twisted in his arms, small firm breasts against the wall of his chest, nightgown riding up, soft bare bottom against the hardness of his groin.

They explored each other's mouths with desperate thirst while their bodies strained to join, be one. All thought was lost in the heat of desire. His hands were everywhere, sliding up her back, round to her breasts, down to her buttocks, between her thighs. Then, still seated, they shifted until she was kneeling, her legs straddling his as he dragged her nightgown over her head and put his mouth to her breasts and began to suckle on her nipples with a hunger matched by the yearning noises she made.

When he finally entered her, it was with gentle, skilled fingers. She was already damp with desire and her body closed round him in spasm, then opened and shut like a flower as he pleasured her to the point of orgasm.

She moaned when he suddenly stopped and pushed her away slightly. Then she opened her eyes and realised.

Lucas had unzipped himself, taking out flesh that throbbed painfully in long denial. She made to touch him, to offer him the same satisfaction, but he caught her hand. He was ready to come and wanted, needed to be inside her.

Tory wanted it, too, shifting with him as he went to the edge of the seat, uncoiling her legs, tilting her hips until he was able to touch his swollen flesh against the soft, moist lips of hers. Then he lifted her slightly to push inside.

Tory didn't expect it. Not the first exquisite pain from the intrusion of his manhood, nor the pleasure that followed. She was gasping with it as he raised her to meet his thrust, bracing herself against his legs and arching back to accommodate him, crying aloud each time he pierced her to the core until they came together in a blend of agony and ecstasy.

She collapsed against him, naked in his arms, stifling a sob of fright that she could feel like this, riven yet complete, fractured yet whole.

He tried to soothe her with gentle kisses, hugging her to him, whispering, 'I've hurt you. I'm sorry. I didn't mean to.'

She shook her head against his shoulder rather than tell him that pleasure overwhelmed her, that love for him was her undoing.

'Shh. Shh. It's okay.' He half carried her to the bed, then lay down beside her, stroking the unruly hair back from her face, brushing a tear away with the back of his fingers. 'Do you want me to go?'

Tory shook her head again and looked at him with sad, dark eyes, unable to express her true feelings.

She wanted him to love her.

He did. After they'd lain together for a while, still on the bed, then wordlessly begun to touch, he loved her the way he knew so well. This time slowly, infinitely gently, undressing to feel the glide of her soft, curving body against the slick sweat of his, learning each part of the other, tasting fingers, toes, the most intimate places until pleasure was a long drawn sigh that left them too high to talk.

Yes, he loved her—if only with his body.

They slept and woke with the sun to make love again and lie, content, in each other's arms. That was how they were discovered.

By Alex.

They had ten seconds warning at most.

Tory heard the outer door opening, thought it imagination, then heard it shutting.

They both heard the tentative knocking on her bedroom door.

'Tory, are you back?' Alex called softly and, eliciting no response, stuck his head round the door.

They weren't caught in the act, but close enough. Tory had managed to sit up, grab a sheet and clutch it to her front. Lucas merely leaned back against the headboard, naked.

Alex took in the scene, too thunderstruck in the first instant to say a word.

When he eventually did, it was a somewhat anticlimactic, 'R-right.'

Tory frowned darkly. She didn't feel anything was right. Spending the night with Lucas wasn't something she'd intended sharing with Alex.

'Boss.' Alex actually nodded in Lucas's direction, before leaving with a 'Excuse me. I think I'll go make coffee.'

'Curious,' drawled Lucas when Alex finally bowed out the door, barely able to hide a grin. 'He took it amazingly well, wouldn't you say?'

'I...yes.' Tory supposed she should explain and turned to do so.

'Perhaps he's gone off searching for a loaded shotgun. What do you think?' Lucas lifted a brow in her direction.

'I think you know,' Tory countered.

'Know what?'

'That Alex was up in Edinburgh, hoping for a reconciliation with his wife.'

'But if *you* knew—' Lucas cut across his own question and, staring hard at her, answered for himself, 'You couldn't care less, could you? Which probably means one of two things— you and Alex are finished, or you and Alex never started.'

'The latter.' Tory didn't see any point in keeping up the pretence. She'd used Alex merely as protection against ending up in bed with Lucas—pretty ineffective protection as it turned out. 'He was broke and homeless so I took him in until he could find somewhere else.'

'Like a stray dog?' Lucas commented dryly.

'Quite,' Tory agreed, 'only a dog would probably be more house-trained.'

Lucas smiled at the acerbic comment. It wasn't directed at him, after all.

'So has he found somewhere?' Lucas was still not happy at the idea of Alex's proximity, however platonic the relationship.

'No, and I can hardly kick him out now.' She sighed in

exasperation. 'Not if we're going to get any sort of promise out of him to keep quiet.'

'About?'

'You and I. In bed. Together.'

She spelled it out for him although she didn't really think it necessary.

He astounded her by replying almost casually, 'Do we have to keep it quiet?'

'Yes, of course. I can't possibly go on working at Eastwich with everyone knowing that you and I are…' She searched for the right words.

'Are?' he prompted and when she didn't come up with anything, suggested, 'Living together?'

'We're not.'

'We could be.'

Tory stared at him in surprise. He'd asked her before but that was so she'd move out on Alex. Now that was hardly necessary.

'Why not?' he added simply, and, catching her chin with one hand, tried more effective persuasion.

The kiss quickly threatened to get out of control and Tory pulled away, shuffling to the other side of the bed to drag on a T-shirt and jogging bottoms. She didn't need sex clouding the issue.

He followed suit, dressing in his clothes from last night, but all the time talking her round. 'You could come stay with me. I've bought an apartment in town. You could keep this place and sublet it to Alex. You can always get the sanitation department in when he vacates,' he finished on a wry note.

'I don't know.' Tory wasn't averse to the idea. She wanted to be with Lucas. But it seemed a giant step. She'd never lived with a man before, not even her ex-fiancé.

He came round the bed to take her in his arms and, smiling down at her, ran on, 'I have nice clean habits, always replace the top on the toothpaste and put the toilet seat back down.'

It wasn't the most romantic of propositions but it made Tory smile and she nodded, thinking she could later change her mind.

She should have know better, of course. With Lucas things tended to happen yesterday.

'You finish dressing and I'll go speak to Alex,' he announced and padded out to the living room, still in his bare feet.

When she later emerged, feeling a little shy, it was to find the two men chatting over a breakfast of beer and corn chips—all that Alex had bought in—having already settled arrangements.

Tory scarcely believed it and remained much in the same state until four days later when she moved into Lucas's trendy loft apartment sited in a warehouse by the river.

For a while it continued to seem unreal to her, eating and sleeping and rising with Lucas before each going off in their separate cars to Eastwich, careful to maintain distance. That proved easier than she could have hoped, as Alex kept a discreet silence before eventually leaving for a new job with BBC Scotland, and his impressive replacement plus a new Lucas—appointed programmes director made contact unnecessary between her department and senior management. Given an almost free hand, she was increasingly confident about her documentary on the so-called bonding weekend and had followed it up by actually interviewing some of the participants—including Amanda who had chucked in her job to fulfil a long-held ambition to write a novel.

She still worked alongside Simon but he was deeply involved in his own project and, with Alex gone, had turned into a demon workaholic with no time to be curious about Tory's private life any more.

That life was something else. At home, they laughed a lot, Lucas and she, and talked endlessly, greedy to know each other, their thoughts, dreams, fears and failures. She learned what those occasional nightmares were about—sights witnessed, the dead and dying, bombs missed, the bullet that hit, during his time as a correspondent. She reciprocated with tales of her childhood—ordinary everyday horrors of maternal abandonment followed by reconciliation, good times with her mother's boyfriends, bad times with not so nice ones. She wasn't looking for sympathy and neither was he. They were explanations of how they had come to this point, the events that had shaped them before they had met.

He cooked and she ate. They shopped together. He fixed things and she tidied. Someone else cleaned. They went out at times but mostly stayed in. They made love, often.

In time it became normal life. She stopped analysing it and worrying there was no future in it and just lived it.

And was happy—deliriously, amazingly, joyfully happy for four wonderful months—until one day the sense of unreality returned.

Lucas noticed her distraction straight away, but wasn't sure if he wanted to discover the cause. He just knew that he'd made her happy all these months and suddenly she wasn't. She continued to make love and let him hold her when it was over and fall asleep in his arms, but when the day came she was restless and anxious and evasive, and, like a coward, he didn't ask why.

A week passed before Tory finally told him. She'd considered concealing it as long as possible but that seemed dishonest.

'There's something you should know,' she announced over the dinner table, then followed it with a lengthy pause.

She'd been rehearsing the words all day but getting them out was something else. She half expected him to comment, *That sounds ominous*, but instead he sat, eyes fathomless, mouth unsmiling. He couldn't already know, could he?

No, she was being fanciful. She decided to tell him the whole story in the hope he might understand and at least forgive.

'When I was a child,' she began quietly, 'I had leukaemia. I was ten and I was treated with a combination of chemotherapy and radiotherapy which—'

'What are you saying, Tor?' Lucas's face was ashen. 'The cancer's returned?'

'No. No, nothing like that. I'm completely cured of it,' Tory assured him hastily. 'I'm sorry. I'm telling this badly...' She took a deep unsteady breath before going off on another apparent tangent. 'Do you remember outside Charlie and Caro's, when I said I'd never have children?'

He nodded, blue eyes fixed intently on her.

'The thing is—' she licked dry lips '—such treatment for cancer has the side effect of making people infertile.'

She paused, giving that fact a chance to sink in. A range of emotions passed over his face, too quickly for her to really read, before he murmured, 'The way you said it, I thought it was a lifestyle choice.'

'I probably gave that impression,' she admitted, 'but, at the time, I didn't feel obliged to go into detail.'

'And since?' he challenged.

Tory hung her head a little. She'd had several chances to tell the truth but had ducked them. 'I was afraid you'd dump me.'

'Because you couldn't have children?' An angry edge had crept into his voice. 'You don't think much of me, do you?'

'Charlie Wainwright dumped me,' she said in her defence.

'That's why you broke up?'

'Pretty much.'

He frowned darkly. 'I suppose you kept it from him, too.'

She nodded. 'At first. But then I didn't see us as a long-term thing.'

'You became engaged,' he reminded her heavily.

'We were at a New Year's party at his parents'.' Tory wanted him to understand how it had been. 'Loads of people there and, out of the blue, Charlie proposes in front of them all. I should have said no, I accept that now.'

Lucas also knew her well enough. 'Only you didn't want to embarrass him?'

She gave a nod, before conceding, 'I guess I fancied it a little, too, the whole package. Up till then Charlie's mother had been pleasant enough to me and his father was really nice and there were so many of them, Wainwright cousins and un-cles and aunts. You felt it was a real family, that you'd almost be part of a dynasty... Do you know what I mean?'

'I should.' Lucas gave a dry smile. 'I was an in-law for four years, remember.'

'Yes, of course.' Tory had momentarily forgotten his first wife had been Charlie's sister.

'I was similarly seduced,' he admitted, 'being also an only child from a single parent set-up. But the Wainwright clan can be claustrophobic after a while, and too dependent.'

Tory realised he was referring to his own experience with the Wainwrights and raised a questioning brow.

'When I married Jessica,' he went on to explain, 'I was earning a relatively modest salary as a correspondent. She couldn't manage to live on it, nor did she want to, and she couldn't see why we had to when her parents were willing and able to supplement it, not to mention my wealthy stepfather... Call it male pride but I didn't like taking handouts.'

A shrug dismissed it as any big deal but his tone had said something else. Like all marriages, his and Jessica Wainwright's had been less than perfect.

'I appreciate that,' Tory said supportively.

He gave her a brief smile. 'One of life's ironies, I suppose, that I eventually did make it, but at the time money was our greatest source of conflict.'

'But you were happy, by and large?' Tory asked.

'Mostly.' It was a measured response, qualified by, 'Not the way I've been with you... You know I'm in love you, don't you, Tor?'

It was the first time he'd used the word love. Another of life's ironies. A week ago she would have wept with joy at it.

'Don't, Luc!' She knew he might take it back all too soon. 'Not till I'm finished saying what I have to say.'

'I thought we had. You can't have children,' he stated baldly. 'I can live with that.'

It wasn't what Tory wanted to hear.

'I can't,' she replied quietly.

His eyes narrowed. 'I don't follow.'

'I...let me explain it all,' she ran on. 'So Charlie and I got engaged and I tell him the truth next day. I don't know what I expected. At any rate, *he* couldn't live with it. His branch of the Wainwright family depended on him, so I let him off the hook.'

Lucas saw her eyes reflect painful memories and reached across the table to cover her hand with his. 'Well, I for one am glad you did. Who needs kids?' He made a dismissive gesture.

It cut through Tory like a knife. She hadn't finished her story but she couldn't now. It was pointless, unfair even.

'So we haven't a problem?' He raised a hand to cup her cheek.

The tenderness in the gesture almost undid her. But he was right. *We* didn't have a problem. *She* did. Not his fault at all.

'No,' she agreed.

'We can go on as we are,' he added.

Tory could have nodded. So much easier to lie. But she suddenly felt sick to her stomach.

'Excuse me.' She rose to her feet as she realised she was actually going to be sick. 'I have to…'

She couldn't think of any invention so she just took to her heels down the corridor to the bathroom of steel and glass. She didn't bother locking the door. Making it to the bowl in time seemed more important.

When Lucas tracked her down, she was still leaning over the sink, the cold tap running as she washed her mouth out. She sensed him behind her and glanced into the mirror to catch his image.

'I can't say I've ever had that effect on a woman before.' Lucas hid his true feelings behind humour.

'It's not you.' She straightened and immediately felt dizzy.

He saw her sway and, catching her arm, led her to a window-seat. 'Just the prospect of continuing to live with me.'

She shook her head. 'I do love you,' she admitted softly. 'I just…just feel trapped.'

'You're lying,' he accused. 'Trapped doesn't come into it, not when you love someone.'

There was a bitter note to his voice that Tory had never heard before. Perhaps she deserved it but she really couldn't cope with acrimony in her current state.

Tears sprung to her eyes and slowly, soundlessly, slid down

her face. She didn't look at him but she heard his exasperated sigh.

'For God's sake, don't cry on me, Tor... Here.' He handed her a tissue from a box on the shelf.

She used it to wipe her tears but more just replaced them. It wasn't the first time in the last week that she'd been a helpless weeping mess—or the first time she'd thrown up.

'Look, I'm sorry—' he bent to kneel at her side '—but I've let down enough women gently to read the signs. I need you to be straight up and honest with me. Just say the words: I don't love you, Luc. Then one of us will pack a bag—me, for now—and we'll shake hands and wish each other well.'

He tipped her chin up so he could see her face. She tried really hard to make it easy on them both. Got as far as 'I don't lo...', then couldn't go on.

He must see the truth in her eyes, anyway. She adored him. Was absolutely, irrevocably, painfully in love with this man.

'Please don't...' She appealed for him to understand.

Lucas didn't but he still put his arms round her and held her and rocked her until her crying subsided.

Tory clung to him, her resolve weakened by his show of compassion. She couldn't leave him. Not today. Tomorrow, maybe. Or some time later. When it showed.

For now she wanted to go on loving him, making love to him as, tears dried, she turned her head and sought his mouth with hers.

Lucas let her kiss him. Began to kiss her back. Lifted her up and carried her to their bed. Sought oblivion in her sweet, slender body. Found it too for a few precious moments.

Then he lay there, watching her catch her breath, rediscovering for the hundredth time how beautiful she was to him, and said words he promised himself he wouldn't.

'Stay with me, Tor—' He just stopped short of begging. 'Give it another chance. I'll—'

Tory put a hand to his mouth, unable to bear it and finally used the truth as a weapon to stop him.

'I'm pregnant.'

She didn't add to it, didn't need to. It hung between them like an exploded bombshell that left silence in its wake.

This time the emotions crossing his face were all too readable. Shock. Disbelief. Anger.

'Run that past me again,' he demanded at length.

She repeated simply, 'I'm pregnant.'

'You can't be.' Not half an hour earlier she'd told him exactly that. He sat up away from her in the bed. He couldn't look at her and think straight.

Tory sat up, too, leaning back against the pillows.

'I know I can't be, but I am.' She'd found out this week, although her body had been showing the signs for months. 'The doctors were wrong all that time ago or maybe it was a chance in a million and I got lucky.'

'Lucky?' He glanced round to challenge her choice of word.

'Yes.' It was how she felt, even now when his, 'Who needs kids?' had told her how *he* would feel. 'I've spent half my life thinking I'd never have children and now this.'

'You're keeping it?' he added.

'Yes.' She'd never considered otherwise. 'I didn't plan it but now it's happened, I'll live with it. That's the reason I'm leaving. I can't and don't expect anything from you, Luc.'

They had once briefly discussed contraception. He'd offered to be responsible and she'd claimed to have it covered. The mistake had been hers.

He twisted round fully and misread the mute apology on her face. 'It's not mine, is it?'

Tory hadn't anticipated such a question. Wishful thinking? Or did he genuinely believe she'd been unfaithful to him?

She shrugged. 'If that's what you'd prefer.'

'Of course it isn't!' His voice rose with his temper.

But Tory felt too emotionally fragile for a slanging match. She shifted to the edge of the bed and, picking up his discarded shirt as a shield, stood up.

He followed, making no attempt to hide his nakedness. In fact, he took the shirt from her nerveless fingers and threw it on the bed. Then he stared at her, down at the slight curve of her belly.

Tory trembled at his intensity then actually flinched when he put the palm of his hand above the place where their baby was growing.

'It's mine now.' He stroked her flesh.

The most intimate of acts without being remotely sexual. 'I—I don't understand.'

'You're mine,' he told her, 'so it's mine. Simple. Just like I'm yours. What happened before we were together has no significance.'

Tory finally caught up. He thought she'd come to him already pregnant. And now, here he was, lying through his teeth—she knew fine he hated the idea of her with another man—so he could keep her.

'I do so love you, Lucas Ryecart.' She wanted him to know that. 'But it's not going to work. "Who needs kids?" Remember? That's what you said less than half an hour ago.'

His brow creased, as if he couldn't recall ever thinking such a thing, far less saying it, even as he admitted, 'Okay, I said it. But what do you expect? The girl I'm planning to marry has just told me she can't have children. So I tell her I want four? I don't think so.'

'Marry?' Tory repeated in a slight daze.

'The sooner, the better, don't you think?' he countered.

Tory still looked at him in disbelief. 'Isn't that rather conventional?'

He grimaced. 'These days conventional is: the man runs out on the women, leaving her holding the baby. I'm assuming that's what he's done.'

'Who?'

'Whoever.'

Tory could have been really mad with him but for the facts a) he was willing to look after her and the child, regardless, and b) she loved him, also regardless.

'My last lover was a sports commentator who worked for ITV,' she began to recount.

'I don't think I want to hear this.'

'Well, tough! Just listen. We had a brief, rather tepid affair that ended amicably when he went off for a month to cover the World Cup.'

'But that was a couple of years ago?'

'Quite, and I'm three months pregnant.'

He looked confused but Tory decided to wait until the penny dropped by itself and, feeling a bit absurd arguing naked, went to pick up her clothes from the floor.

Lucas watched her dressing, then dressed too, but on automatic pilot as the true situation dawned on him.

'It's my baby.' It was a statement this time.

Tory turned and awarded him a somewhat cheeky grin. ''Fraid so, but there's always plastic surgery.'

'It's not funny.' For once Lucas wanted a serious conversation.

But Tory felt skittish. He'd asked her to marry him! He'd asked her to marry him while thinking she was having someone else's baby! What other love token did a girl need?

'So why did you let me believe otherwise?' he demanded, trying to remain angry with her.

'Not guilty, your honour,' she threw back. 'I said, "I'm pregnant." You said, "It's not mine, is it?" I rest my case… I'm starving. Fancy some supper?'

He looked ready to explode at the change of subject but Tory was too happy to care as she walked back through the living area to the kitchen beyond. All week she'd fretted over his reaction. She still wasn't sure precisely what it was but telling her he loved her was certainly an improvement on what she'd visualised.

He trailed her through, still arguing the toss. 'But why else keep it a secret? Why not tell me earlier? You knew days ago, didn't you?'

'I thought…' she paused to sort it out in her own head '…you'd imagine it was deliberate. That I'd got pregnant to trap you. I felt bad, too. You'd made it plain you weren't planning on children and I said I had it covered. I really did think it was impossible, you know?'

He nodded, accepting her word, and realised how each had

misread the other. 'In point of fact, kids were part of my five-year plan.'

'Five-year plan?'

'First year you live with me. Second year, I convince you to marry me. Third and fourth we consolidate. Fifth, we reproduce.'

He ticked each off with a finger and Tory was left wondering if he really could have thought that far ahead.

'I've wrecked that, then.' She grimaced in apology.

'So, things will happen a little quicker.' He shrugged and, coming round the side of the breakfast bar, put his arms round her waist from behind. 'And money isn't a problem so you can choose whether to take a career break or hire a good old British nanny or work part-time if the boss is amenable,' he ended on a wry note.

'And is he?'

'Very.'

It was banter but Tory added more seriously, 'Is he really? To fatherhood, I mean.'

'Hell, yes.' He grinned back. 'If I wait much longer, I'd be too old to swing a baseball bat.'

'Cricket bat, you mean,' she couldn't resist correcting. 'Anyway, it could be a girl.'

'Either one will suit,' he replied and Tory didn't have to see his face to know he was smiling.

She turned in his arms all the same and reached up to kiss him on the cheek and say, 'Thank you.'

He slanted her a quizzical look. 'What was that for?'

'Making it all right.' Tory still couldn't believe her luck.

'*All right?*' he echoed and laughed aloud. 'It's goddamn wonderful!'

And Tory finally trusted it was real, the life of happiness stretching before her, coloured vivid by the man at her side.

The world's bestselling romance series.

HARLEQUIN®
Presents

Seduction and Passion Guaranteed!

Legally wed, great together in bed,
but he's never said…"I love you."

They're…

Wedlocked!

The series
in which
marriages are
made in haste…
and love
comes later…

Don't miss

THE TOKEN WIFE by Sara Craven,
#2369 on sale January 2004

Coming soon

THE CONSTANTIN MARRIAGE by Lindsay Armstrong,
#2384 on sale March 2004

Pick up a Harlequin Presents® novel and you will
enter a world of spine-tingling passion and
provocative, tantalizing romance!

Available wherever Harlequin books are sold.

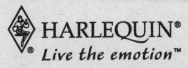

HARLEQUIN®
Live the emotion™

Visit us at www.eHarlequin.com

HPWEDJF

The world's bestselling romance series.

Seduction and Passion Guaranteed!

They're the men who have
everything—except a bride…

Wealth, power, charm—what else could
a heart-stoppingly handsome tycoon need?
In the GREEK TYCOONS miniseries you have
already been introduced to some gorgeous
Greek multimillionaires who are in need of wives.

THE GREEK TYCOON'S SECRET CHILD
by Cathy Williams
on sale now, #2376

THE GREEK'S VIRGIN BRIDE
by Julia James
on sale March, #2383

THE MISTRESS PURCHASE
by Penny Jordan
on sale April, #2386

Pick up a Harlequin Presents® novel and you will
enter a world of spine-tingling passion and
provocative, tantalizing romance!

Available wherever Harlequin books are sold.

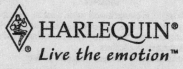

Live the emotion™

Visit us at www.eHarlequin.com

If you enjoyed what you just read,
then we've got an offer you can't resist!

Take 2 bestselling love stories FREE!

Plus get a FREE surprise gift!

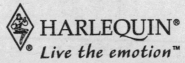

HARLEQUIN®
INTRIGUE®

Our unique brand of high-caliber romantic suspense just cannot be contained. And to meet our readers' demands, Harlequin Intrigue is expanding its publishing lineup to include **SIX** breathtaking titles every month!

Here's what we have in store for you:

❑ A trilogy of **Heartskeep** stories by Dani Sinclair

❑ More great **Bachelors at Large** books featuring sexy, single cops

❑ Plus outstanding contributions from your favorite Harlequin Intrigue authors, such as Amanda Stevens, B.J. Daniels and Gayle Wilson

MORE variety.
MORE pulse-pounding excitement.
MORE of your favorite authors and series.
Every month.

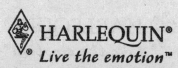

HARLEQUIN®
Live the emotion™

Visit us at www.tryIntrigue.com

HI4T06B

The world's bestselling romance series.

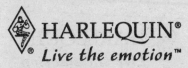